# A Gypsy's Thief

## Titania Ladley

ELLORA'S CAVE
ROMANTICA PUBLISHING

# *What the critics are saying...*

## ဆ

**5 Angels and a Recommended Read!** "A Gypsy Thief is a very scorching hot book. The erotic scenes will leave you fanning yourself and wanting more. [...] Ms. Ladley has left this reader wanting more of her books. I can't wait until the next book comes out and Ms Ladley's books are a keeper for any reader. I would recommend this book to anyone who likes fantasy and erotic. You will not be able to resist its pull!"
~ *Fallen Angel Reviews*

**5 Stars!** "Titania Ladley has done it again! Many praises for her creative story and her talent for bringing characters alive off the pages. She has a way of emotionally connecting the reader to the story, it's characters and the time period it's written in. She has a writing style that isn't to be missed. The story itself grabs you and doesn't let go keeping you entertained from beginning to end. I couldn't quit turning pages until the end. I highly recommend this series and this book is a definite "do not miss. Highly recommended." ~ *Euro-Reviews*

**5 Blue Ribbons!** "A GYPSY'S THIEF: THIEVES AND LOVERS by Titania Ladley is scorching hot. John and Catriona cannot keep their hands off each other and the erotic scenes between them will leave the reader sweating and squirming in their seats. Ms. Ladley has always left her readers wanting more in her books and each time she has delivered to them. I highly recommend this book for your shelf; however, be sure to have a fire extinguisher on hand to put out the fire. Also,

Ms. Ladley is one of the featured authors on the Romance Junkies website." ~ *Romance Junkies*

An Ellora's Cave Romantica Publication

www.ellorascave.com

A Gypsy's Thief

Electronic book Publication June 2006
Trade paperback Publication January 2008

# Also by Titania Ladley

**ઠ**

A Wanton's Thief

Bat Scratch Fever

Curse of the Black Widow

Enchanted Rogues (*anthology*)

Heads or Tails?

Jennie in a Bottle

Me Tarzan, You Jewel

Moonlite Mirage

Naughty & Spice

Spell of the Chameleon


### Writing as Roxana Blaze

Shades of Passion

# About the Author

❧

Titania Ladley knew it was necessary to hang up her stethoscope forever and write fulltime when her characters started coming to work with her on the graveyard shift. A pretty scary prospect when a nurse is unable to tell the difference between patients, spirits and her over-active imagination. So for the benefit of mankind, Titania clocked out one morning after working a grueling twelve-hour night shift and dragged her persistent characters home with her. She marched in the door, tossed her bag of medical paraphernalia into the spare bedroom and put her trembling, tired hands to the keyboard. You bet she was scared out of her booty! But there was just no other way for Titania to live — nor was there for her patients. ;)

Happily, Titania's never looked back. Residing in Minnesota with her very own hunky hero, one child remaining at home and twins in college, Titania devotes her spare time to family, reading erotic romances, walking, weightlifting, crocheting and baking fattening desserts. And arguing with her stubborn alpha males and kick-ass heroines.

She also writes under the pen name Roxana Blaze.

Titania welcomes comments from readers. You can find her website and email address on her author bio page at www.ellorascave.com.

## Tell Us What You Think

We appreciate hearing reader opinions about our books. You can email us at Comments@EllorasCave.com.

# A GYPSY'S THIEF

છ

# Dedication

ॐ

*To Zachary, a handsome, chivalrous knight in his own right. I love you!*
*And as always, to my wonderful editor, Briana St. James — thanks so very much for your continued support, expertise and guidance.*

# Dear Reader

ॐ

In A Wanton's Thief, my first in the Thieves & Lovers series, I took you on a journey of fiery, erotic romance during the days of King Henry VIII's court. Immortal bandit Falcon Montague — aka Robin Hood — and the spunky but demure Salena Tremayne found eternal love by the hand of fate, channeled through the wizard Lorcan. But what of Little John who shared an energizing triad with his soul-brother and Lady Tremayne? Will he find a love destined to be his and his alone, or is he doomed to live his immortal life seeking soul-fueling companionship only when necessary? Fast-forward to the time of Scottish ruler, King James VI, hell-bent on eradicating his kingdom of witches. Again, destiny must dictate, and Lorcan's ulterior but secret motives are becoming more urgent for the mysterious wizard. In A Gypsy's Thief, the second in the Thieves & Lovers series, I return you to a time of chivalry, magic and a burning love between a Scottish Gypsy lass and John Lawton, aka Little John, of Robin Hood's band of thieves. Enjoy!

# Chapter One
*February, 1592*

**❧**

*Northern England near the Scotland border at the height of the*
*North Berwick witch-hunt skirmishes*

"Get the witch, ye fools! Get her *now* or face yer own executions!"

Horses' hooves thundered upon the snow-packed earth, sending up a powdery, white cloud. John Lawton lowered his longbow where it had been aimed squarely at an eight-point buck poised but a score of yards across the clearing. He whipped his head around and took stock of the sudden flurry of activity that burst from the copse of woods.

"Do not let her get away, I say!" It was one of the knights of Scotland's ruler King James VI, apparent by the style of his armor and helmet. Except for one lone soldier watching from afar at the rear of the troops, it seemed this warrior, perched regally upon his massive steed, was the only member of the king's faction of any worth. Surrounding the lead man in current command were dozens of poorly suited soldiers with little to protect them against the chill of winter. Their mounts appeared to be in just as dire need of nourishment as the riders.

*How pathetic that the king would not invest more richly in his own army but instead enlist these poor excuses for soldiers to take up arms against an accused "witch".*

John's scrutiny shifted to the rear of the small army. He studied the man-at-arms hanging back as if in gloating command of this ragged party. Though the distance kept John from seeing the face, he noted the plaid the man wore, as well as the dirk, sword, helmet and armor not of the English crown. The small brigade was obviously Scottish, he was certain by the thick brogues and the glaring kilts worn by only the first- and second-in-command. But had this company of sentinels truly crossed this far south of the border just to pursue this one harmless looking fellow?

John's gaze swung to the hooded and unmounted figure racing through the snow with naught but thin leather riding boots upon his feet. He appeared to be well fed, almost chubby, but John could not see his face or body. The large brown robes and cloak he wore concealed all but the condensation of his ragged breaths churning out from the cave of the darkened hood.

Apparently, it seemed, the army had the wrong person, for the one dubbed a female witch appeared to be all bulky man. The quarry veered to the left around a towering oak and straight across the meadow toward John. The hunted man sprinted with the agility and speed of a lad half his bulk yet as he neared, John heard the wheezing of a person long on the run and in dire need of rest.

"Draw yer bows," shouted the one in present authority. "Fire!"

The soldiers obeyed, notching then raising their ragged weapons. John tightened his grip on his own bow and arrow and raised it in defense. "You! Get behind me at once!" he ordered of the fleeing suspect.

Too late. He had heard John's voice and apparently assumed him to be one of the pursuers, for he arced back toward the woods. A shower of arrows rained through the air, led by one from the silent ruler at the rear of the pack. The young man grunted and stumbled through the snow when one struck him at a hard angle. The shaft embedded in his right breast.

"Excellent! Go now and fetch the devil woman this instant and return her to the scheduled burnin'." The gloating knight in current charge whirled his mount. He made a show of reining in so that his Friesian reared up and pawed the chilly afternoon air with a neigh and a snort. "The commander and I will await ye all at MacLacklin Hall, in the name of the King of Scots. Off with ye! Make haste, I say!" And he shot back into the forest, he and the one John assumed to be the commander in plaid, racing away from the skirmish.

John heard the moaning and gurgling. The victim now hunched in the blood-dappled snow. He clutched his chest where the arrow's tip exited. John had not the faintest hint what this man—or rather, "witch"—had done to deserve this, but it was high time he put an end to this brutal madness. With the exception of expeditious travel through *invisilation*, rarely did he use his sorcerer's skill of speed. However, this dire situation called for drastic measures.

With lightning quickness, he loaded, released and reloaded arrow after arrow. The ungodly swish-and-snap tune proved far less astonishing than the rapidity at which he executed his weapons. His marksmanship and the velocity of his ammunition rivaled that of an entire deluge of the king's finest defenders. The iron-tipped spears met with implacable accuracy in each soldier's hand or shoulder. Howls and screams rent the crisp winter air. Blood spurted onto scraggly nags, dribbled down to soak the white earth.

"Go, every last one of you," he shouted as he set another arrow for fire. "Return to your king and deliver him a message, if you please. Tell your ruler I—a newly acquired, vengeful enemy—will do all I can to prevent such heinous witch-hunting practices. If this man dies...your king dies."

A collective gasp echoed in the meadow.

"Who may we say speaks such a treasonous vow?" The largest of the remaining warriors urged his mount forward.

"Though I am not of your country to be rightfully classified as traitor, I implore you to relay my name to your king. They call me Little John of none other than the League of Thieves."

Silence lingered. A falcon flew overhead letting out a sharp caw of warning.

"Ye be of the bandit Robin Hood's thieves? Nae, it cannot be."

John nodded, one eye and ear trained on the wounded man at his right. He continued to rock and moan with both hands fisted protectively around the arrow at his chest, guarding its movement with his frail life. John knew time was of the essence, that he needed to get these henchmen on their way soon or the poor man could die.

"Aye, one and the same. The dangerous, vengeful bandit who sees all, knows all...seeks revenge upon all those who cross him and who take unfair advantage of the less fortunate."

A moment of hushed fear and awe hung heavy in the air as the winds moaned through the woods. The fallen victim's gurgling breaths became shallow and rapid. They blended eerily with winter's blustery tune, a foreshadowing of death to come.

"We now depart," one scrawny knight announced with celerity and a shiver of misgiving. He waved a bloodied hand to the others and spun his mount around. "Men, without further delay, retreat, I say!"

"But what of the witch..."

"Leave her. Do ye not ken who this mon is? Do not be a fool!"

Alertness boiled deep in John's veins. He scanned the remaining men. Half of the soldiers hesitated, while the others turned and darted into the woods. John raised his loaded longbow and aimed at the skinny one who appeared to have regained his bravery and become their new leader.

"You have already been witness to my swift...talents," John drawled lazily. "It would take but one single second to bring each and every one of you down. And this time, I can guarantee I will not avoid your vital organs as I purposely did the first time."

He heard an agonized groan and darted a furtive glance at the "witch". The man toppled over at that very moment and flopped onto his side. The scarlet puddle beneath him slowly widened reminding John of red wine spilling onto a pristine white linen tablecloth. John heard the familiar wheezing tune of one struggling to breathe through a punctured, fluid-filled lung. His heart did a flip behind his breastbone. He had to get to the man before death overtook him or John's healing powers would be useless.

"The king shall hear of this, ye ken?" the soldier warned as he tugged his roan around.

"While I do not doubt that one small measure, I am counting on it. Now, begone with you all!" He released an arrow and sent it whizzing by the rider's head. The man ducked, but not soon enough, for he let out a yelp when it grazed his ear. John did not give the witch-hunters time to acclimate themselves to his offense. With precision born centuries ago, he showered the band of men with another round of arrows.

"Retreat, men!"

John persevered until every rider disappeared and the beat of hooves died down, fading into the thick forest. The only sounds left were the winter breeze whistling through the gnarled tree limbs and that of the gasping figure curled on the snow nearby.

John tossed his bow across his back and raced to the man's location. He now lay on his left side, the hood of his cloak covering his face. The iron tip, along with a hand's length of wooden arrow, exited at the right breast near the armpit where an alarming amount of blood soaked the cape and the snow below him. Yet John knew he still lived by the occasional puff of white breath and the gurgling respirations. But the young man did not appear to have much longer.

He knelt in the snow before the wounded man's chest, heedless of the cold and wetness permeating his braies. "Lad, you must hold very still while I remove the arrow."

The figure merely groaned followed by a racking cough. John saw blood trickle down the pale jaw, the only portion of the man's face visible under the sagging hood. Closing his eyes, he leaned forward over the limp figure. He wrapped his right hand around the portion protruding from the inside edge of the lad's right lower shoulder. Pressing his left hand against the man's back with the arrow jutting up between his fingers, he snapped off the excess length of the foreign object.

The young man screamed, his body twitched. More blood seeped forth and coated John's hands. He dredged up his powers of healing and forced the warm-cold medicinal energy to pour forth and penetrate the lad's back. Gradually, the blood trickled to a dribble, leaving a maroon splotch on the brown cloak.

"Easy, now. I'm going to roll you onto your back and pull the remainder of the arrow out. The cold of the snow will hopefully cease the blood flow temporarily and ease your pain."

A moan of protest gurgled through the restriction of the blood-filled throat.

"Man, I will not let you die. It must be done. Trust me. I will be able to complete your healing once the arrow is removed."

John knew he must hurry if the stranger had any chance at survival. Against wails of objection, he rolled him onto his back. The body flopped over with an agonized growl. John noted how the bulk of it felt much lighter than anticipated. It did not take long for an explanation to stare him right in the face.

"Lorcan alive! It *is* a woman." His heart slammed behind his ribs. In that one instant, his entire existence spiraled out of control. Beautiful eyes glittering with pain and unshed tears filled John's vision making him gasp for his own breath of air.

*Green. As green as the meadow on a crisp spring morn'.*

His own words came back to haunt him, words spoken over fifty-five years ago to Falcon and Salena Montague. No, John could not deny that the large eyes rimmed by black-fringed lashes were an exact match to the *Scorpian*. The old wizard Lorcan had begun to wear the *Scorpian* medallion shortly after removing the *Centaurus* and granting it to Salena Tremayne. Falcon's own immortal life's omen had been established and guided by the *Centaurus'* fate. Salena had been wearing the stone ever since to impart youthful immortality to herself in order to remain at Falcon's side for eternity as his wife. It now nestled between her lovely breasts due to Falcon — and some unknown pre-determined chance — claiming her as his intended decades ago. Not to mention because of the exact match of her eyes to the stone, and her perfect birth time and order to the stars.

It was definitely apparent this was no lad. Long wisps of silky, raven hair escaped the hood of the cloak, the wavy tips now soaked deep red with her own blood. Her face was that of an angel's, heart-shaped, delicate, almost regal. Beneath the faint gray-tinged complexion of one who has lost a dangerous amount of blood, John could detect a naturally dusky, caramel tone to the smooth skin. Its hue shone in contrast to the rich mane and unusual shade of eyes. Could this woman be descended from the hundreds of foreign *Rom* tribes, that of the Gypsies known to roam the Lowlands?

Interest piqued, he moved the caress of his gaze from the jarring green pools, down the pert little nose to the lips now shivering blue with cold and loss of blood. Her creamy neck stretched slim and elegant, like that of a princess descended from royalty. John could almost imagine the silky feel of it against his lips, the fragrance of her skin wafting up to taunt him as he ravished her. The taste of her sweet flesh, the sight of her naked —

*That's enough, Lawton! Guide your thoughts elsewhere. This cannot be what it seems. You will not* allow *it to be such. And you will preserve her life* now!

He jerked his stare to the chest area where the arrow pierced between ribs and collarbone, finally making a lethal path through skin and thick linen.

*Get on with it, John, before she dies.*

He lifted his hand and pressed it against the wound surrounding the arrow's exit. Aye, he felt the soft swell of her upper breast beneath the thick folds of fabric. Obviously, the maid had been attempting to disguise her feminine sex from the witch-hunters. In addition to adding needed warmth, she had wrapped herself in layer upon layer of robes and cloaks, most likely in order to disguise and fatten her image and round herself out into a plump young man.

But John dallied no further. The young lady lay dying before his very eyes.

"Lie still. This may hurt, but I promise you 'twill not be for long."

Her eyes flared with fear. She gasped raggedly and dug her boots into the snow, struggling to wriggle from John's reach.

"Nae, please..." she rasped, and John's heart ceased its immortal life beats. The husky, sultry tone laced by the song of a Scottish lass gave him mental pause. Yet he continued quickly in his healing process before the lady's panic caused her own death.

"I say lie still," he repeated more sternly this time. After a period of useless, weak struggles, she obeyed, but he did not miss the snap of anger that overrode the pain and terror in her gaze.

John rose up on the balls of his feet, squatting at the young female's side. He held one hand against her chest at the base of the arrow and wrapped his other around its wooden shaft. Pulling with one quick motion, he felt the sickening sensation of her lung giving way to the scrape of a foreign object and then to blessed, empty space.

The woman screamed, her shrill outcry echoing eerily across the forest. She twitched, her dainty hands slapping the reddened snow at her sides. Her eyes widened, the spring green orbs rolling back in her head. Without further delay, John tossed the broken arrow over his shoulder and knelt again, using his weight to press his hands upon the gushing wound.

He inhaled and held his breath, knowing due to the extensive damage, this would be one of the most draining, difficult healing processes in his entire existence. He clamped his eyes shut and imagined each injured piece of tissue, the nicked lung, the torn flesh and grazed ribs. John channeled his energy through his hands and focused its cold-hot powers deep into the woman's chest. As the minutes passed, he could feel the flow of blood righting itself, the gurgle of air through the punctured lung fading as the woman's breathing passage became cleansed of all blood.

Already, his energy waned. This lifesaving task was just too draining, sapping what strength he had left within him. He had already used much of his powers by releasing the arrows in rapid speed, and by healing the entrance wound at her back. He felt the familiar dizziness wash through him, that of depleted stores and a need for power-replenishing sex. But the job was not yet done, for he could sense the remaining torn tissue within the depths of the right breast. While she now lay unconscious but breathing normally, he could mentally perceive that the hole beneath the garments remained as an ugly, gaping wound.

"Concentrate, man. Finish healing her."

John kept his blood-soaked hands in place and struggled to complete the task. His body trembled as he fought to feed the curing strength into her. But he had depleted a large portion of his stores. Perspiration trickled down his spine, foreshadowing further dangerous diminishment of his soul.

His hands no longer tingled with energy, and for the first time in days, he experienced the biting chill of winter as it permeated his fingers to the very bone. Exhaustion overtook him and finally, he gave into it, slumping over the young maid's body.

* * * * *

Catriona Graham regained consciousness at precisely the moment her lungs filled with the woodsy aroma of man. Soft, long hair the very color and depth of a midnight sky tickled her nose. If it were not for the warmth the man cocooned her with, she would have screamed to bloody hell by now and thrown him away. Her backside felt in need of a good spring thaw. Oh, but her front side where her heart nestled inside her chest, it pumped with hot blood!

She glanced down and tried to recall how she had gotten in this precarious predicament. But her thoughts detoured while her gaze beheld the rugged face of a god. He was not unconscious, for his eyes were open, though they appeared somewhat glazed with fatigue as if he fought the clutches of oblivion. Lord God, but they were like twin gems of iced sapphires with a faint twinkle of something altogether baser! If it were not for the look of weariness in them, she would have been certain her body had responded with swift desire.

But that was impossible. She had mourned the death of her beloved husband Duncan for the past nine months. Not once since King James had ordered him burned at the stake in North Berwick for suspicion of witchcraft, had she felt even an inkling of want for any man. No. Never. She trusted no one, for it seemed everyone who had befriended her since Duncan's death had been a spy of the king who had set out to destroy her as well.

And why not? She could hardly blame them. The Scots king offered a fortune to all who assisted him in eradicating those suspected of witchery. Therein lay the problem. *Suspected.* No trial, no explanations allowed, no exceptions.

Which was why she had fled North Berwick weeks — or had it been months? — ago in disguise and made her way south to the English border. That fateful night of her flight, she had been caught by the townsfolk while performing her séance ceremony in order to reach Duncan. It had not taken her long to gather her meager belongings — which she had since lost or been forced to abandon — from the cottage and escape into the frosty night.

"Ah, she lives." His voice came out in a backwoods English lilt, jarring her from her thoughts. It strummed her ears and made her shiver.

"Who are ye?" Catriona's tone sounded a bit more alarmed than she cared to reveal. After all, it appeared she lay pinned beneath a stranger — perhaps one of the king's tribunal seminarians in pursuit of her? She struggled to remember how she had gotten here on the ground beneath this man, but all she could recall was running for her life, searing pain and then...jumbled nothing. She had no idea who this man was and why he sprawled across her. But she would not be taking any chances. She had been fooled too many times in the last months to let her guard down yet again.

No, Catriona had learned her bloody lesson for the last time.

"The name is John. John Lawton, at your service," he murmured, but he made no indication he intended to move.

Ignoring the warning thud of her pulse in her ears, she wiggled in an attempt to shift his massive bulk off her. "Ow!" A vague soreness arced through her chest. "Sir — Mister Lawton — I demand that ye remove yerself from me person. Begone with ye — *now*."

His mouth curved into a rakish yet bitter grin. She caught a glimpse of straight rows of white teeth, as white as the snow that blanketed the countryside. "Oh, if only 'twere possible."

Feeling cornered and extremely alarmed, she took a quick glancing sweep of her surroundings. The snow had been disturbed extensively over near yonder copse, most likely by a large group of horses' hooves. That was when she remembered...

She had been discovered by the king's search party while hiding out in a shallow rabbit burrow just five score of yards away opposite this leg of the forest. Apparently, her disguise had not fooled the old sheep farmer she had sought refuge from a mile back. He had tipped off the sentries and it had only been sheer luck that a young lad had happened upon her shortly before she had been detected and warned her of what hovered on the horizon. She had made haste and run for the dense woods in hopes of being concealed. But, determined as they were, they had found her anyway.

And they had pierced her clean through the lung with a sharpened arrow. Catriona remembered well the agony and terror of it. She gasped and glanced down at her chest. Somehow, the arrow was gone, but a slight tenderness remained on the surface. She could distinctly recall the unbelievable pain of its entry, the hot, wet gush of blood within her garments, drowning in her own blood and fighting for air, a voice shouting at her...

*"You! Get behind me at once!"* Yes, she recalled now the shouting had sounded much like this man's voice. In her rush, she had assumed him to be one of the king's murderers. She had veered off in the other direction, and that was when the arrow had struck its intended mark. Catriona had begged God for her last breath, could vividly recall the bright red snow pooled beneath her while she faded in and out of consciousness, fighting for every breath of air.

So how, then, could it be? She gaped down at where she was certain the arrow had protruded from her breast before she had fainted. A ragged, bloodied hole in her cloak appeared to be the only evidence she had not dreamed the agony of the arrow's penetration and the trauma of near-death. Alarm rang through her, making her quiver like the huge bell being struck within the kirk near her home in North Berwick.

"God almighty, have I died?" Her breath came out on a bubble of panic. Squirming, she tried to push him away, tried to peer around his head to view the angels she could swear she heard strumming harps. "Please," she groaned, tears stinging her eyes. "I am too young to die."

Confusion at her miraculous healing and the distant music she heard, prompted her to call upon spirits of the dead. If anyone could verify her life status, they could. She clamped her eyelids tight and focused, chanting, calling to the other side.

"Oh spirits, hear me call. Please, please...hear me call." But not one soul channeled to her. The usual eerie voices rang back deafeningly silent in her head, and the typical tingly sensations and cool bursts of air up her spine did not occur.

"Spirits?"

She gasped out loud, ignoring the man's puzzlement. Lord above, maybe the inability to reach them meant she *was* dead? She still did not know for sure if this man had truly been wily foe or gallant defender. And if she had passed on, did she really need to fret over it one way or the other? Perhaps *he* was an angel causing the ghostly tunes to reverberate in her head? He certainly could pass for one, though with his dark and sometimes brooding looks, he more resembled a *fallen* angel. As she perused his fine bone structure framed by all that dark hair, she suddenly realized the music was nothing more than the wind whistling through the trees. And she now lay vulnerable beneath him in the wilderness with naught but the small dagger in her boot for protection.

He chuckled a deep song of amusement. The pleasant timbre of it yanked her from her alarm. It made her relax a small measure. "I have not a bloody clue in hell what spirits you mumble in regard to, but nay, you most certainly are not dead." His gaze swept her from lips to breasts, now threatening to spill from within her man's shirt due to the oaf's weight pressed upon her. The constriction increased when her heart thundered at that smoldering look. She glanced away, reminding herself to elevate the importance of escape above all else.

"I will be dead if ye do not get yer bloody bulk off me." She punctuated that with a wiggle and a grunt.

*Now, Catriona. Ye must escape now!*

"We are not done here, my — "

"Verra well, I will not say it again." Catriona drew up one knee and shoved away the many thicknesses of robes and cloaks. *Fallen angel entity or living man*? she mused. *We shall see, Catriona, just which one you have become entangled with.*

Her fingers fumbled at the sagging edges of her man's braies where the long leggings had been stuffed into her leather boots near her calf. With the swift speed of a murderess, she wrapped her hand around the dagger's ivory handle and snapped it upward. His chin remained resting on her chest, but she was still able to maneuver and twist her wrist so that the cold blade's edge pressed against the man's throat.

"Remove yerself from me person now."

He did not so much as flinch. "I cannot, lest you…"

The longer he delayed, the more the fear clutched at her gut and seemed to intensify the slight pain that throbbed in her chest. She had never sliced a man's throat before now, and did not relish the idea of engaging in such a gory task even when her life depended upon it. But she *would* do it if worst came to worst.

"Lest I?"

"Lest you…kiss me."

She blinked. Her gaze narrowed on his, shadowed there beneath his feathered woodsman's hat. Yet she saw nothing but seriousness in his liquid-blue eyes. "Pray tell, *what* did ye say, mon?"

"You see, milady, it seems my energies have been sapped by healing your mortal wound. If you but kiss me, I should have enough power to rise and whisk you off to safety and a warm shelter."

She started to laugh but the discomfort proved too much to bear. "Ye're utterly daft."

"Nay. 'Tis true." He actually shrugged. "But 'tis your choice if you wish to lie here and freeze to death."

"I am goin' to inquire just one more time, sir." She increased the pressure of the knife at his neck. "Just who—I mean truly *who*—in God's holy name, *are* ye?"

He did not seem the least bit daunted by her weapon, though she watched as a tiny drop of blood pearled against the blade. Watched and struggled to suppress the nausea it stirred within her abdomen.

"Ah, did I not already inform you? Aye, I believe I did. 'Twas at the beginning of this awkward conversation. Well, I suppose I shall repeat myself. I am John Lawton, referred to by some as Little John."

Catriona tried to focus, while his arrogant tone did not go unnoticed. The man's name echoed in her head as his image wavered before her. Her heart palpitated, thumping behind her breastbone and making her gasp for air. "Little John, as in…the Englishmon of the thief and murderer Robin Hood's band?"

"Aye, one and the same."

"Nae, it cannot be…"

"Oh, but it can and 'tis. Our delightful, merry tales have moved through the centuries…as have we."

"Lord God, save me from this bloody murderer!" Catriona squealed and managed to wriggle her body out from under John's torso, despite the vague pain it caused her. She rolled, dislodging the knife from her grip, and came up on her knees clawing her way through the snow and out of his reach.

But his iron-hard hand clamped around her ankle before she could leap to her feet and run. "Lady, do not make me further expend what energy remains. I repeat, you *will* kiss me…lest you wish to possibly see an immortal man truly die."

Her panicked gaze located the dirk, but it was too far out of reach. She tried to extend her free leg behind her to kick him, but he spun her around so that she plopped onto her rear. It afforded Catriona her first glimpse of the enormous red splotch soaking the snow. Since awakening, she had not taken note of the exact spot where she had been lying. *Nae, ye fool. It seemed ye allowed this mon to bewitch ye into oblivious idiocy.* Oh, but Lord forbid, she had now regained her senses. The atrocious, sickening sight of blood rent a moaning gasp from her making her forget she had been in the process of escape. Her stomach churned with queasiness.

Catriona's hand came up and she clamped her teeth over her knuckle. "Nae…nae…"

"Oh, aye, your own blood it be, lass."

"B-but how? Where is the arrow? I recall the attack, the arrow lancin' me back." She looked down again at her red-drenched cape, felt sharp cold air nip at her flesh through Duncan's ripped doublet beneath. And again, Catriona saw all the evidence of her inevitable death except the arrow she was now certain had spent her blood. "The arrow, 'tis…'tis gone. And other than a wee bit of tenderness here at me breast, I feel well. H-how can that be?"

She studied the stranger, watched intently as he pondered his next words. Varied, imperceptible emotions flickered in his striking eyes. Her gaze swept the length of his body, now spread across the snow in a half-sprawl, half-side-lying position as he continued to hold her ankle. He was fit and bonny with muscles bulging beneath his sleeves, and there was no doubt his physique would be considered exceptionally pleasing to any woman's eager touch. The glimpse of wide shoulders and tight, jerkin-clad chest she saw through the gaping opening of his cloak made her hands fist involuntarily.

She accepted in one indiscriminate glance his dark handsomeness and virile, enormous presence could prove enough to bring any maid to her knees in a swoon. But stunning looks aside, his fitness became the more prominent trait, evidenced by the strong grip he had around her ankle and the stubbornness he bullied her with. It served to remind her even a godlike man such as this one should be discounted as a woman's possible suitor. Therefore, if he insisted on using his barbaric talents on her, she would insist on resisting his innate charms.

It seemed he chose to wield his manly powers after all. Determined, despite his temporary weakness, he dragged her closer...closer to the pool of bloody snow.

"What, milady? Are you telling me you do not recall being disencumbered of the arrow, being rescued by a gallant knight?" His slash of eyebrows arched mockingly. "A gallant knight—" he nodded his head in lieu of a gentleman's bow, "who remains at your service as we speak?"

His words brought it all back in its entirety—the terror of being hunted to the brink of death, the unbearable pain of the arrow hitting its mark. Next had come the panic and the inability to draw air into her lungs, and the subsequent suffocating and drowning in her own blood. His image warbled before her as truth warred with disbelief in her head. Gods alive, the man had truly healed her?

"Eh?" he demanded when she could only gape at him.

"Nae, I tell ye it cannot be..." She collapsed onto her back, ignoring the snow's coldness blanketing her backside. Catriona stared up at the crisp blue of the winter's sky and watched as a single crow flew across her vision and cawed almost derisively. Her breath came out in clouds of white from her mouth, clouds of life, she thought disbelievingly. Having performed miracles herself by bringing the dead back to engage with the living, she knew such prodigals did exist. And yet it seemed difficult to accept when on the receiving end.

Now that she allowed her mind to replay what he claimed, Catriona could remember in fuzzy bits how he had, indeed, removed the deadly arrow from her chest. She could recall it as if it had been a nightmare, the agonizing rip of the foreign object from her body, the insufferable torment followed by the cold-hot feel of his touch, the gradual lessening of pain and the relief of drawing air into her lungs. And finally the blessed blackness.

A tremor went up her spine. "Are...are ye a sorcerer then?"

He tilted his head and grinned boyishly, an innocent smile far from that of an ogre who might dabble in black magic. "And are you—the accused and practically sentenced witch—denouncing me a wielder of witchcraft?"

*Nae*, she said calmly to herself. Far be it for Catriona Graham, gifted seer into the world of the dead, to doubt the talents of others also gifted. Now that she had had the time and this man's jogging of her foggy brain to recall just what powers he held—and how he had even used them on her—she possessed no further skepticism as a "normal" person might. Aye, it still boggled her mind and made her tremble in awe to be in the presence of a true warlock. But there was no need to *appear* to give in so gullibly to him, to lose what upper hand she may possibly gain.

She lifted her chin. "Och! What ye have done—yer magical healin' with those large hands of yers—'tis far from the realm of reality as most ken it."

"Most? But not you, milady?"

She hated that he seemed to see right through her. And she hated that her lad's disguise had not fooled him, that he saw her definitively as a female.

"What does it matter, I ask ye? Nae, never yer mind," she amended with a blink. "Come to think on it, I kindly request that ye release me leg. I must be on me way before they return."

He cocked his head as if a thought had just occurred to him. "What is your name, lass?"

"That, sir, is none of yer bloody affair."

"Nay, I relish knowing the names of those I intend to kiss. Call it rubbish if you will, but 'tis a very bad obsession of mine."

"And I've already informed ye... *I will not kiss ye!*"

He shook his head slow and deliberate, narrowing those mystical orbs on her. "Such a selfish proclamation from one whose life has just been restored, who has just escaped the clutches of death via my healing hands."

Guilt assailed her like the drenching of a cold spring rain, but she swiped it away. "'Tis no gentlemon ye be to seek a lady's guilt for yer own end. I would say it seems there be a spot of selfishness on yer part, as well, Mr. Lawton."

"John, if you please. And I do see your valid point. An eye for an eye," he growled, gasping for air as he dragged himself up and over her.

Instantly, his woodsy scent assailed her nostrils and filled her lungs—saturated the very lung he had just repaired. She looked up to see perspiration glistening across his forehead and knew he struggled for every bit of energy he expended. Though she sensed his apparent distress somehow related to his powers, the novelty of it—of him—continued to awe her. *Why* he had become so weak was yet to be determined, but the truth of his plight stared her in the face with stubborn desperation. She accepted that his request for a kiss was not, for the most part, a ploy to take advantage of her. It struck her as apparent and genuine that he truly sought her out to energize his mystical powers. She had heard of such a rare phenomenon for some but she had yet to witness this borrowing of energy to gain strength. The truth was, he had given her life and vigor, and it was now time to repay her debt to this magical man. But her thoughts about witchcraft and the supernatural scattered when she looked deep into his crystal eyes.

Deep into his soul.

Her body trembled, though not with the cold. He rendered Catriona temporarily speechless, for his rugged, dark beauty stole her words from her throat before she could retort. Oh, this man was definitely a wizard, no doubt about that now. But was he truly one of the infamous outlaw Robin Hood's cohorts? The mere possibility sent a thrill of excitement through her she cared not to address.

She had to get away, had to continue running past the Scottish-English border, otherwise, his life-saving measures would be for naught. It was imperative she make her way to London where she would be under the jurisdiction of the queen and be afforded the opportunity of anonymity in London's busy streets. She would be blissfully lost in the safety of crowds a whole country away from North Berwick and the witch hangings void of a trial—and the fiery stakes the king insisted on igniting.

She extinguished the horrid memory of tortured screams and the putrid odor of burning flesh in her mind...that of Duncan's cries and her own mother's as well. Instead, she focused on this man who fascinated her so very much against her better judgment. Despite his obvious weakness, he still seemed to have her at a disadvantage both physically and mentally. But perhaps it was time to outwit him by striking up a bargain with the big oaf?

"Oh, aye, I do so agree...an eye for an eye. What say ye I grant ye the kiss ye so desire...in exchange for me freedom?"

He chuckled, throwing his head back so that his long ropes of hair fluttered in the breeze and settled across his shoulders. What would it feel like to run her fingers through the long tresses? Just trying to imagine it made her fingers tingle with an alarming want. Duncan had kept his auburn hair in a severe cut that swung against his jaw. This man's hair...it appeared much thicker and fell unconventionally long down his back. It gleamed with a healthy sheen she had never before seen in her husband's unkempt locks.

"I would think that as a witch, you would not need to lower yourself to such bargains."

"Would ye, now? Well, I would be thinkin' that as a sorcerer, ye would not need to be lowerin' yerself to stealin' kisses from a helpless maiden."

He snorted. "I'd hardly call you helpless, given the fact that, based on your lovely Scottish brogue, you have come a long way all alone and dressed in your male disguise as you are. Now *that* takes strength to be a female in a man's clothing, to flee one's country and king's wrath and *still* be alive—up until the near-fatal strike of that bloody arrow, that is. Indeed, that impressive strength of yours does not even account for the constant strain of having the king's paid men bearing down on your tail all the while."

She snorted back. "Methinks I shall take that rather long-winded repartee of yers as a bloody good compliment."

"Mmm," he said on a nod, his eyes twinkling with a glimmer of something altogether hot and mysterious. "'Tis definitely a compliment."

The tune of his voice so close to her ear, along with his cryptic expression, made her clit suddenly engorge with blood, while a gush of pussy juices soaked into the crotch of her braies against her will. The pressure of his lower body to hers increased as he relaxed, a move that brought his codpiece flush to her vee. Her legs had been slowly spread by the gradual weight of him, and the intimate position brought a hot flush to her cheeks. Catriona could feel the unmistakable hardness of his sex even through the thickness of his garment, as well as through her own clothing. The sensation of a swollen male organ between her thighs—a long-forgotten memory in the months since Duncan's imprisonment and execution—washed over her with ruthless speed. Memories assailed her of what it once felt like to be breathless with lust, to give up in beautiful, submissive abandon to the talents of a passionate man in need of a woman.

Of a woman in need of a man.

*Enough, Catriona!*

"Och, get on with it, thief." Catriona forced an exaggerated tone of insolence into her voice. "Steal yer kiss just as ye and yer Prince of Thieves continually seize the riches of the innocent and all their poor bairns. Please hurry, be done with it, and then I expect ye to free me posthaste."

He stared so intensely into her eyes, she could have sworn he had already seduced her and brought her to climax in that one instant. "First, I must hear your name from those plump, delectable lips."

She ignored the way his words and his deep, sensual voice thickened her blood, stilled her heart's thumping. "Me name?"

"Aye," he rasped, raking a hand across her hood to release the remainder of her locks. "Your name, love."

Love? The endearment did odd things to her insides. A wanted criminal now combed his fingers through the blood-soaked tips of her hair, and it made her eyelids go heavy, her spine tingle. What had gotten into her? Had this thief—this wizard!—cast some sort of carnal hex on her?

The sarcastic answer she offered John was, "Verra well, sir. Ye win. I am called Catriona Graham with former fealty to the clan Nicol."

"Where are you bound?"

"Bound?" She scoffed. "To bloody anywhere away from the forest of blazin' stakes in North Berwick! I flee, good sir, from me beloved Scotland, from all I have ever known as me home. I could ill afford to remain in that place of danger much longer. It has become a ferocious hell for those cursed with any one of many gifts of the supernatural. The Scottish king, he goes on a dogged mission and cannot be convinced otherwise 'til he sees all those with...talents, dead. So do ye not see, brute? Death continues in me pursuit and surely awaits me if ye do not let me go."

She paused awaiting a reply, or at the very least, a protest to the insult. When one did not come forth and he only raised a brow at her, she went on. "Now, please, I demand that ye allow me to pay me bloody debt so I can be on me way this instant."

His cool eyes warmed, reminding her of a steeping cup of water tinged with the slightest bit of juice from a blueberry. Catriona dropped her gaze to his wide mouth where it now curved into a rakish grin. Her hand itched to slap the leering smile from his face, but her mouth watered, despite that violent urge. She licked her lips almost instinctively. Aye, it had been so long since she had been kissed by a man. Reluctantly—though she would rather burn in hell than admit it to him—she supposed she would not mind getting just a minute sample of that beautiful mouth of his...

"I wholeheartedly accept payment."

His cryptic words kindled a wave of expectancy through her blood. Bargain now sealed, John lowered his mouth, slow and deliberate, until his lips barely met hers. She had not expected the bargain to get underway so quickly, nor had she expected her own swift surrender to those talented lips. Warm, soft, powerful, all things irresistible and pleasant bloomed in her mind. The wet energy that rained down tender on her mouth left her spellbound, and she realized she held her breath, waiting, anticipating...what?

Unfamiliar, delicious flavors burst in her mouth making her open up to accept his tongue against her mind's better judgment. He increased the pressure and entered her mouth with maddening slowness. Catriona's heart leapt into a gallop and she could swear that lethal arrow had pierced her chest once again. She inhaled his rugged scent and nearly sighed when he sighed, when he shifted and gathered her body up against the solid wall of his chest. Her nipples sprang to life, even through the thicknesses of male garments. A vague inferno ignited between her legs, spread upward through her torso and limbs and combusted into an unexpected, long-forgotten need that frightened her.

And Catriona realized in that one moment she had sorely erred by allowing this bandit, this sorcerer, to wield his black magic upon her unsuspecting heart.

# Chapter Two

ဆာ

John spiraled into the swift clutches of lust, of utter, sweet madness. He could swear he kissed the very petals of a rain-dappled rose. The silky, moist softness, the tart flavor bursting into sugary syrup as he delved deeper, made him go hard with the feral need to sink himself between her thighs.

He sighed at the familiar vibrations of his soul reviving. It always started deep in his abdomen and fanned out from there. Though this one kiss would do little to sustain him for long, the pleasure through consummated intercourse, or some form of sexual release, was the main conduit of revival. But since the kiss proved even more arousing than he had guessed it might, it should be enough to get him to the next village where he would be forced to seek out the charms of the first wanton maid to offer her services.

It was not John's normal practice to approach his soul revitalization by a mere kiss, but he had unexpectedly expended nearly all of his stores on saving this one wench. It would now be necessary to obtain the energy as quickly as possible. If only Falcon and Salena were nearby. They would be glad to oblige him, which would energize Falcon—or Robin Hood—as well. But John did not have enough reserve left to perform his usual speedy *invisilation* travels to their most recent location near London. He had been out on a leisurely hunt on the border, and his own closest manor was south of here near York, some goodly distance from his current position. There was no other way about it. He would be forced to obtain—at the very least—just enough from this saucy siren to gain the energy to rise and go seek out stronger, longer-lasting vitality elsewhere.

Catriona let out a tiny whimper into his mouth. Her arms slithered across his shoulders and around his neck. *Hmm…perhaps I* could *get a bit more power from her than originally anticipated?* A longer, more passionate kiss than expected might do the trick more so than he had expected. If his powers were more like Falcon's, he could simply be on his merry way devoid of rejuvenation and await a subject to provide him what he needed later.

As it were, neither a sword sharpened to a hair's width, nor a man's strong chokehold, nor even the tip of an arrow shot right through his heart had the power to destroy John. Instead, he had been cursed with the one and only handicap that could bring an immortal of his kind to his grave. The inability to function to full capacity without constant replenishment.

He sighed and shook the gloomy thought from his mind, taking advantage while he still could, of what this vixen now offered him. Her sudden surrender gave him hope and increased the throbbing in his cock. John inhaled, taking in the scent of the cold season mixed with warm woman. Though he was certain it had been some time since she had been afforded a bath due to her extensive on-foot winter travels, he could still detect a pleasant fragrance that was all aglow with pliant female. He longed to rip the men's clothing from her and unveil what treasures hid beneath all those layers. Ah, to be free to gaze upon her creamy skin, to sample its flavor and unique texture…

But he had bargained for merely a kiss, and by God, that was all he would take…for now.

Her upper body tightened as she drew him down and plunged her tongue into his mouth. He groaned, loving the way her long legs relaxed and widened, inviting him to press nearer. John could detect the outline of her curves beneath him, the full swell of bosom and hip. It made him all the more curious and suddenly bent on gaining more of that energy from her than first planned.

The deeper and longer she kissed him, the more energized he became. His core trembled, reviving and resonating throughout his every cell. Father of Zeus! If her kisses alone had the power to give him this much strength, what would happen if he were allowed into her warm quim to spill his seed? Would it be different than any other woman in his long past? Would he experience this same profoundness he now did by a mere kiss, only multiplied tenfold—or more, perhaps?

The ridiculous thought had him shivering and made him once again think of the *Scorpian*. It currently resided around Lorcan's neck. According to the eccentric wizard, it awaited John's imminent discovery of his true mate. To that, John always had one response. Bah! The old man and his bizarre mumblings had plagued him for centuries. Despite Falcon and Salena's miracle with the *Centaurus*, *Scorpian* or no, John refused to believe such inconceivable fantasies of a daft old wizard. But curiosity had him lifting his eyelids. He cupped her small face in his palms, willing her to open her eyes as well. He needed to see those gems again, to examine them and ensure their similarity to the *Scorpian* was simply a coincidence.

Her thick black lashes fluttered open even as she deepened the kiss. The glazed passion in the heavy-lidded orbs made him groan again. John stared intently into the emerald pools, so like the *Scorpian*...almost *too* much so to be real.

Nay, it could not be. He could not ever be for sure unless he were given the chance to hold the stone up next to the dazed eyes that now held him captive. Even if afforded the opportunity, it was an utterly bizarre idea to think a man could find his soul mate just by matching a gem on a medallion to a pair of eyes. He did not know what Lorcan's motivation was for attempting to find him and Falcon each a lifelong mate, but frankly, he did not care. He would not get himself involved with any capricious woman ever again, whether the eyes were a dead match to the *Scorpian* or not.

John continued to hold her face as he tasted the flavor of her, like warmed cider on a cold winter's night. He examined the tiny rim of darker green around both irises and pupils. Did the old man's medallion have the same characteristics?

He let out a long breath and tore his mouth from hers, knowing it was futile to debate it at this moment. What did it matter? He would not, under any circumstances, be repeating the courting process ever again. John had experienced heartache brought on by women in his long past he cared not to admit even to himself. He did not wish to attempt permanent association with this or any other woman again, *Scorpian* or no. Unlike Falcon, John's opposition to women was rooted in his continual experience with rejection. He had a decided knack for scaring off the ladies and finding himself in the position of being jilted. Smitten with requited love on many an occasion, it had simply taken his large cock sunk within their passage and his voracious appetite to frighten them off. Salena had been the first woman in centuries to be able to physically handle him — and even *welcome* him and his enormous tool on a fairly regular basis!

"Well?" She spoke through her teeth, her chest rising and falling beneath his. A mixture of bravery and passion — or was it fear? — glowed in her wind-pinkened face.

Nay, this woman would be no different than all the others, he thought as his gaze drifted down to the glistening, bruised lips. All it would take with her would be one encounter. Just like all the others, she would flee in panic, a thief riding off into the dark of eternity, trampling his pride and his heart. Best to just take what he could from her and move on to the safety of what he had had to resort to of late — a more experienced lady of the evening to replenish his stores. One he would not expect a long-term emotional commitment from.

Either way, he would fight whatever rubbish Lorcan insisted on, whether it proved to be true destiny or not. John Lawton was no simpleton. He would be a fool to believe such a crazy phenomenon as Lorcan's ramblings of "fate", of all things!

Despite Falcon and Salena's apparent good match, and in spite of the wonder of John's own magical powers, he refused to believe in the idea that one person in all the universe was destined to be his. Falcon—lucky fellow—had found true love in every past era and not once been jilted. But he had resisted Salena for fear of having to re-experience the heartache of watching a loved one grow old and die before his very eyes. Now that Salena wore the *Centaurus*, life everlasting was hers, and Falcon had been gifted with a devoted, loving mate into eternity.

But nay, John had not been so lucky. So he would just gather the stores of energy he needed from this woman and move on to the next. His gaze swung upward, back to the sparkling twin gems, and regret marred his energized mood. No need to torture oneself with unnecessary emotion. Unnecessary emotion, even if the eyes seemed to possibly match the *Scorpian*, and had the power to take his immortal breath from his lungs.

"Well?" she said again, this time with a mocking blink. "I've offered up me end of the bargain. 'Tis now yer turn. Shall we get on with it, brigand? I've not got time to be dallyin' any longer."

Ah, but of course, she must have felt his humongous erection. Which equated to time to fly the roost, just like all the others. "Mmm, yes, time is of the essence—the fact that the Scottish king's men seek your beautiful head upon a platter. Now *that*, I must say, is an exceptional reason not to prolong the initiation of the kiss."

"Prolong it, ye say?" Her voice came out as indignation laced with that lovely Scottish brogue. The sharp inflections and animated rise and fall of the tone entertained and drew on his senses like the lovely serenade of bagpipes. The soft burr so very close to his ear enchanted him and made his body thrum with need.

"Come to think on it, sir thief, seems the kiss," she went on, "was more than what ye bargained for. I already paid me bloody debt tenfold."

"Oh, aye, 'twas most certainly more than I bargained for. I feel more energized by just one of your sweet kisses than by the full run up a maid's skirts. What is it, *bonny* lass, that makes you possess such power?" He narrowed his eyes, a thought suddenly occurring to him. "Hmm, did that daft old wizard Lorcan send you to me?"

"Lorcan? Who in the farthin' hell is Lorcan?" She did not wait for an answer but went right to the attempted flight. Her arms flailed. She managed to swipe a stinging palm across his cheek. "Let me *go!*" She grunted when he merely tightened his arms about her.

*To hell with her, John. Why put yourself through this madness? You have enough energy to get you to the next village. Let her go and then wash your hands of this she-cat forever.*

He was just about to loosen his hold on her and rise when the arrow struck him in the back. John gasped, not from pain but from surprise. Like a fool, he had allowed this woman to remove his focus from impending danger. When he angled his body just enough to look over his shoulder to locate the source of the arrow, another struck.

But this one did not embed safely within his immortal, invincible flesh. Once again, Catriona had been hit...and this time, right through the heart.

* * * * *

Catriona would always remember the odd range of sensations, from the bliss she had experienced by his kiss to that of her heart being pierced. As excruciating pain tore through her chest once again, she fought the clutches of death.

Her gaze moved to his. In those unique, crystal-blue eyes, she saw shock and something altogether touching yet indefinable.

"Catriona..." She must have been delirious, for she could have sworn she detected affection within the deep tone of his voice. "Do not die—*no!*"

The pounding of hooves upon the snow-packed ground echoed around her. Next came the shouts of those evil men set on burning her to death, the swish of more arrows as they sliced through the frigid air. When a soft yellow glow washed over John's handsome face and erased it from her vision, she was left alone in a place of peace. Catriona knew there was little to be done. She would die this day—she *had* died.

As her weightless body floated into nothingness, she could hear the soft song of his distant voice wrapping her in a final blanket of comfort. His panicked tone failed to alarm her, and instead she embraced indifference and a sort of numb serenity. The pain had ebbed, so much so that she no longer dwelled on the unbearable fire that seemed to have been previously ignited behind her breastbone.

"Mighty powers of magi, of oracles, of great. 'Tis my wish to protect this maiden, to *invisilate*."

He hummed a song of heaven so faint, it seemed to melt into her soul. Strong arms encircled her body even as she left it. Catriona catapulted into an oblivion thrumming with energy, light, warmth. She might have likened it to a lover's blissful touch were it not for the fiery pain that once again emerged in her chest. The fleeting euphoria she had experienced left her with a jolt. A *snap* sounded, a sickening noise that made her think of a bone breaking. Indeed, she wondered if every bone in her body had just shattered.

*Oh, God above, how it hurts again!*

"Catriona..."

She rolled her head from side to side, moaned when the same cold-hot sensation she had experienced after the first arrow, now soaked her left breast. Catriona exhaled as the pain ebbed. It was the very same relief, the identical wonderment she had felt by his healing touch at her earlier injury.

"Catriona. I command you to awaken."

She heard the crackle of a fire, smelled its hearty burn. Relief and pleasant warmth enveloped her body, something she had not luxuriated in, in weeks. On a sigh, her eyelids fluttered open.

Catriona struggled to bring him into focus. He appeared to be nothing more than a dark splotch at first. Gradually, her eyes adjusted to the muted light surrounding his ruggedly handsome face. Concern lit his smoldering gaze...concern for her, she was sure of it by the worry line that marred his forehead beneath the stray lock of midnight hair. Something...something about it made her heart still as if it had been lanced by yet another arrow.

Drawing in a deep breath, she savored the soothing, icy-hot sensation of his palm kneading what was left of the wound at her breast. She knew he continued to mend her flesh, and though it still filled her with wonderment, she accepted his healing gift as fact. The awe of her acknowledgment of John's gift, and the tenderness in his touch, rendered her speechless. Oh, Catriona had spoken to the dead countless times, but now she could identify with at least part of their state of existence. Though she had not crossed over completely, mayhap it would make her a better, more sympathetic medium in the future? She herself had been the oracle of miracles, the connection to the afterlife for those left behind to drown in their grief. But never before had she encountered such divine revelations, nor been the subject of such eccentricity by another human being.

Indeed, the admission of this fascinating phenomenon occurring on her behalf gave her sudden, suspicious pause. Her abdomen fluttered with a swift wariness that had her blurting out, "I-I must ken this verra instant...who—who *are* ye? And why do ye take such care with me, me but a stranger branded a witch, no less?"

John continued to massage her breast making her mind go to muddy mush. "I have already informed you, milady. I am John Lawton of Robin Hood's —"

"Aye, aye, I am aware of that! But why would a man of such magnificent infamy go to such pains to save the life of a lowly, mixed-breed Scottish Gypsy such as meself? And *twice*, at that!"

His brows dipped. She watched, mystified, as a murderous twinkle lit the pale eyes. But he did not ease up the healing ministrations at her breast. The ecstasy of his touch increased, shifted into something more of a sweet, erotic nature rather than that of a medicinal sort. Indeed, she felt as if she had been stricken with a malady of seduction entwined in sorcery. She had become a captive under the spell of a dangerous soothsayer.

"Were you to meet Falcon — Robin Hood — you would know that nary a single good, honest man or woman is viewed as lowly in his eyes — nor in mine."

Indeed, she had been brought to a place far from a dwelling for the lowly. She glanced around to see that she rested upon a massive four-poster bed, the columns made of French walnut, while the headboard appeared to be of carved limewood. Beneath her, the softness of a feather mattress caressed her backside, and a down pillow cradled her head.

Her gaze moved farther down when his thumb brushed her nipple, and it was then she realized during that strange dream, he had somehow removed her cloak, robes, shirt and jerkin. Naked from the waist up, all that remained of her man's clothing were the braies, codpiece and leather boots she wore. John knelt at the bedside, one large hand continuing to cup her breast. Even as fire rushed through her torso and into her pelvis, her stare jerked from corner to corner of the richly furnished room.

"I'll be wantin' to ken at once, where...where have ye taken me? How did I arrive here?"

"Ah, love, relax. You are safe now. You occupy my chambers at one of my two estates, this one in the Yorkshire region in the far north of England. As far as how, well, milady…" He winked, charming her with little effort, so much so that she could swear the outer layers of her heart thawed. "Let us just say 'tis yet another of my sorcerer's gifts, one of swift bodily movements in which I did just as I promised. Your gallant knight has whisked you away to safety."

"B-but ye claimed not to even have the energy t-to… I do not understand. How were ye able to carry me here to—"

"Not carry, love. Fly…in a sense. Now shh," he rasped, planting a finger against her lips to silence her. "Remain calm while I complete the healing process. 'Tis all right, my lovely witch," he said almost sarcastically. "I will not hurt you. I merely repay a debt. You see, your generous kiss has given me more energy than I ever fathomed from a woman. Ironically so, 'twas that very generosity that in turn saved your own life—in a sense."

"Aye, and I have paid me debts, as well. While I thank ye for yer gift of life, 'tis me every wish to be on me way— forthwith."

His hand tightened, the fingers stroking with adept precision. It caused the slow roll of desire to speed up and pool in her womb. He licked his lips, his gaze moving down to devour her nakedness. Despite the urgency of her words, the sweep of his stare made her long to taste of him once again, to further the madness of this wicked spell. She inhaled, pulling the earthy scent of him into her healed lungs. Her heart fluttered in her chest and she gasped when he pinched an areola between two firm fingers. Across the room in the massive stone fireplace, flames licked higher, sizzling in time with her flesh. Catriona's body tightened like a finely strung bow, poised, ready to be notched and released.

"No need for you to depart…just yet. You are safe here, over a score of miles from those in your pursuit. You've the gift of life within you," he coaxed, his voice as deep and dark as potent wine while he lowered his head to the other breast. "You are simply a wily cat who now enjoys her third life."

"Ye...yer powers..." She held her breath, released it on a moan when his tongue flicked over her nipple and his teeth nipped and pulled. "Ye truly somehow brought me thus far, to a place where no one—not one single soul—kens of me whereabouts?"

"Not one single soul but I, my luscious dove." His hot gaze swept her body. It made her skin tingle with the irresistible desire for his hands to follow in their path.

Normally, his cryptic words would have given her cause for alarm. But not now. Not with his hand sliding down across her quivering belly and into her braies, not with the soothing wetness he so easily elicited from her pussy.

*God, so help me, but I cannot resist this warlock's touch! It has been so verra long...too long since I've felt a mon's hands upon me flesh.*

"So..." she panted, her clitoris jolting when his finger found the pebble-hard knot. "I owe ye...a debt...once again, do I?"

"Nay, you owe me not a thing," he whispered, and the arid breeze of his breath moved along her ribs just before his tongue dragged downward to her navel. "But I will not refuse any further generosity," he announced as he increased the pressure, "you may care to bestow upon me."

He sank that wicked, talented finger into the slit of her soaking mound. She arched off the bed and a cry tore from her depths. "Holy priestess!"

Duncan suddenly flashed in her mind, along with a wash of guilt. But there was simply no comparison, no possible way to force the memories to stay when this amazing man did things—sinful things—to her traitorous body.

"Your fatal injury is now healed...you are healthy, ready. Tell me—I beg of you—allow me to make love to you, Catriona."

He had actually given her a choice, though she knew there to be only one correct, feasible answer. It had been too long since she had experienced the power of a man, that awesome force pounding between her legs, the scents and flavors that could addict a woman while that one stroke of cock filled her to ecstatic madness. Oh, aye, she needed a man desperately, and despite her better judgment, this one would do quite nicely. She trusted him without knowing how or why, knew without a doubt somehow, that the danger of the king's sentinels loomed as but a distant threat.

He groaned, awaiting her reply, while his mouth embarked on a hot trail up and over her previously injured breast. John nipped and sucked his way up the slope of her neck until he reached her mouth. But a breath's space from her lips, he whispered, "Please?"

Their eyes met. Catriona shuddered at the barely restrained glaze of lust in his gaze. Time dissolved into cool nothingness even as her pussy warmed, melting like wax surrounding a candle's dancing flame. From somewhere afar, she heard the sizzle of burning wood, smelled its pleasing yet acrid odor as it mingled with John's manly scent. Intense, unfamiliar emotions assaulted her, twisting at her heart. They were sentiments that she did not know how to name, she realized. She only knew she wanted. Wanted this man.

"Ah, bandit," she rasped, "me handsome blackguard. Ye tempt a widow's neglected libido beyond resistance. Me mind insists on nae—oh, but me wanton body, it screams...aye— *aye!*"

His eyes lit with what she could only describe as relieved desire. "I promise to take care with your wounded widow's heart, to show you pleasures befitting a princess, a royal queen."

She gasped at his kind, seductive words. Though she had had but one man in her bed in all of her score and four years, Catriona Graham was no naïve maid. She knew just what he alluded to.

"Mmm, the honorable words of a dishonest thief, ye be professin'. So irresistible...even to a *witch*." She pulled his mouth to hers, threading her fingers through the thick hair at the back of his head. His sigh melded into her own, into a tune of mutual surrender at the exact moment her heart completed its thaw. Her hand slipped up and joined the other in the silky mass of long locks. Catriona cupped his skull, holding his mouth captive to hers. She tasted a sweet fire that seared her hunger deeper, richer. Oh, and he gave her more as if he had read her mind. His tongue delved into the far recesses of her mouth, dancing, teasing, making a slow, hot path of erotic honey travel from her lips right down into the depths of her womanhood.

His body moved, covering hers from chest to toes. A warm, sensual cocoon enveloped her. She burrowed in, moaning when he gathered her close and settled between her thighs. No longer were the cumbersome robes and cloak between them as had been when first they had met. It was as if the braies she still wore were naught but a thin wisp of air. The heat of his clad body permeated the garments' thickness and soaked into her flesh making her breathe out in audible relief. Allowing a sense of dreaminess to overtake her, Catriona tuned into the distant winter winds as they howled outside the keep. Something about its almost romantic yet baleful tune made her stretch, inhale deeply. She drew in the wild aroma of arousal, danger and savory man. He quite simply intoxicated her with subtle undertones of animal prowess.

How amazing that John had already saved her life twice. She reached for him, marveling at the thought, comparing the kind gesture to his burly, massive presence. *Ah, but what woman could not resist a knight in shinin' armor?*

Not the new Catriona Graham, she determined skimming her palms over the meaty muscle and smooth skin of his back. But he didn't allow her much time to explore. Tearing his mouth from hers, he flipped her onto her stomach.

"I'm sorry, Catriona, but I cannot wait a moment longer. I have to see, touch, taste every inch of you. Now."

Excitement rushed through her veins when he brushed her hair aside and dragged his hands down the length of her bare back and clothed buttocks. It had not taken him long to fulfill his apologetic confession. Every inch of her body tingled with gooseflesh. The muscles in her ass tightened when he cupped her there, but quickly she let go and relaxed, gasping inwardly when his firm movements caused the crotch of her braies to abrade over her clitoris.

"Mmm," was all she could force out. Her body went limp even as her quim throbbed with need. Though she did not move, she felt alive, more alive than she had felt nine months ago before Duncan's execution—nae, even longer ago due to the extended witch-hunt followed by Duncan's lengthy imprisonment prior to his death.

But nae, she could not allow herself to think of such thoughts even if she wished to. This sorcerer exerted his powers of seduction over her with practiced hands. Those very hands drew the braies, codpiece and boots down in one sweep, leaving her bare ass for his perusal.

His eyes bore into her, she could tell by the unmistakable heat of their darkening depths upon the flesh of her backside. She shuddered with hedonistic excitement, never before having been in this position for the intent of lovemaking.

"A portrait of perfection," John declared, his voice deep and syrupy.

At his bold profession, a sudden wave of self-consciousness trickled up her back. She twisted, started to reach down to pull the linens up, but his hand clamped around her wrist.

"Nay. Do not hide such beauty from me. I want to see you. Every gorgeous curve and crevice."

Catriona's hand trembled against his tight hold. God in heaven, what was it about this man, about his dominant yet gentle manner, that made her heart catch in her throat? Glancing down at her captive hand, then over her shoulder at his face, she slowly let go of the blanket. His eyes...they were ablaze with blue flames, alight with barely contained ardor. But the fascination did not end there. Her gaze swept lower down the hard, naked expanse of his body. Somehow—no doubt, via use of his black magic—he had rid himself of his clothing. She could see the enormous, proud jut of his cock. An involuntary, strangled, almost feral cry tore from her throat.

"Aye, I've no doubt you want this tool of mine now," he insisted, one hand moving lower to stroke the very shaft he spoke of. He planted a hand on her spine and guided her so that she returned to the prone position, but she continued to watch his every move over her shoulder. His stare flitted down to her rear where he took his free hand and spread the globes of her ass apart. Warm air caressed her sensitive, private flesh, and she groaned when a sticky droplet of her juices dribbled from her cunt.

His eyelids went limp as he gazed upon her pussy from behind. "Mmm, sweet cream pours from your slit in anticipation."

"Me body has never—until meetin' ye—opposed what me mind dictates. So let it be kent for the record this ease of submission 'twould be the first for Catriona Graham."

"So noted. Your admission pleases me intensely, vixen." He ran a finger up one inner thigh and swiped her lips. She nearly came off the bed at the expert move, but it was when he inserted the sticky finger into his mouth and spoke around it that she nearly lost all restraint. "But let it also be known—for the record, of course—that this will not be the last time while in my company that your mind and body will be at war..."

He dove down and started a nipping, licking path from her heel up to the back of her thigh. Shivers of blissful desire raced up her skin and settled heavy in her passage. Her pussy moistened further, increasing its fluid in abundance, while her clit throbbed in waiting for his touch. He moved up her leg, his hands starting a trail his mouth then followed. John reached her ass, both hands cupping and squeezing, until she thought she would go limp with ecstasy.

"Such soft skin, such a nicely rounded derrière…mmm, such a tight asshole you have there."

Catriona's eyelids had been heavy with languidness, but now they flew open at his cryptic words. She stiffened, recalling stories from other women in the band of Gypsies she and Duncan had traveled with. Stories of men using that particular…hole for sexual pleasure. And women enjoying it.

Despite the sudden tingling in her anus and the increased throbbing between her legs, she squirmed and shouted, "Nae! Do not even think of usin' —"

His chuckle and the light pat on her ass cut her words short. "'Tis all right, Cat. I will never do anything to you that you do not welcome."

The low, level tone to his voice coupled with the intimate, shortened version of her name had an instant calming effect on her racing nerves. The love-tap on her rear did the opposite to her pulse. Somehow, she believed the cad's honest assurance only made her want him more. Long-buried desire burned deep in her core. Her heart and her body had made the decision for her…be damned with the self-wrath her conscience insisted upon! What became uppermost was the fact she was safe from those witch-hunting predators for the time being. Therefore, she would give herself this gift, this loving warmth her widow's sense knew could only be attained through a man's dominant, firm touch. This loving warmth she had grown accustomed to and had once taken for granted. But never again! She needed desperately to savor it once more. Just as her stomach welcomed nourishing food and her parched mouth drank greedily of cool water, so did her cunt thirst to be filled with cock.

"We shall never ken, for at this moment, I welcome yer advances. Bein' a widow, it has left me without a mon's touch for nigh on a year. If I may be so bold as to say, that sort of pain, I tell ye, it can be tryin' on a woman's body and soul."

"Aye, and 'tis with great care I tend to that wounded widow's soul and most exquisite body." He growled it out even as he nipped one cheek of her ass before moving on to her waist, her shoulders. Pinpricks of gooseflesh swept her from rear to scalp. His hands glided along her flesh, molding, worshiping, making her muscles relax while her libido ignited into a ferocious inferno.

"Nay, no lad here, to be sure," he whispered in her ear. He inhaled, sighed. "Mmm, nothing but complete, ripe and delectable woman."

His breathing came hot and deep making her tremble with delight. Sprawled on her belly with her head turned to one side, she could catch bits and glimpses of him as he rained soft kisses across her cheek, her ear, her neck and shoulder. Heat enveloped her bare back when he slowly lowered his weight onto hers, forcing her legs fully apart. She could feel the tickle of his sparse chest hairs as they brushed her shoulder blades. Rippling abdomen muscles blanketed the small of her back, the upper swell of her rear. It made her head spin with excitement to be surrounded and overpowered by the fever and strength of him. It was the sort of tempestuousness only a lover could bring, the sort she had forced into the dark recesses of her mind for nigh on a year. But no longer…

The scent of aroused man engulfed her making her mouth water, her labia and clit engorge. Catriona gasped and clutched at the bedclothes when his penis probed her wet mons, dragging up and down the swell of her lips. The sensation of being filled by a cock seemed an eternity ago, yet she knew precisely what would come. She hungered desperately to be torn into from behind.

"Your wetness…" he rasped, his hands skimming over her bent arms until he could twine his fingers into hers. "It pours out onto the bed like a rushing waterfall in spring, fresh, awakening the new season and putting the winter to rest."

"Do not talk, me thief. Just give me what I yearn for, what I remember to be a pleasin' experience between man and woman."

"Pleasing? Ah, you have much to learn, milady." He finally aligned the tip of his rod with her hole, its silky head barely entering her, stretching her tight slit. It made her suppress a strangled sigh of relief for what was to come, made her insides contract in welcome anticipation. "I will do much, much more than simply please you. I will take you to the brink of madness and never permit you to return."

And he rammed into her making her scream with bliss. A long, beastly groan followed when he dropped his forehead to her shoulder, gripped her hands tighter and struggled to hold still.

"Jesus, Cat, you are so damn wet and *tight!*"

She heard the tone of barely contained restraint in his voice and knew a moment of woman's satisfaction surpassing any in her entire past. It made her grind her teeth together, made her body tense until she shoved her rear up against him to drive him completely into her.

Her eyes widened. Her mouth formed into an involuntary O, and a sort of savage cry tore from her lungs.

"Oh…and ye are so…big! I do not ken if I can…" Catriona suddenly saw the irony in his name. Little John, indeed, she scoffed silently. *Nae, quite the contrary.* Enormous, and yet she surprised herself in being able to take him all in.

She reared back again, amazed when the outer edges of the orgasm already reached for her. But it receded when John stilled his motion, preventing her from repeating her thrusting moves. He taunted her, she was sure of it, making her wonder if he had planned it this way, to dangle ecstasy before her as if she were his trained dog in heat.

"Hold still, filly," he murmured, and a tremor went through him from toe to head.

"Nae, I—"

"Shh," he interrupted, his teeth scraping at her nape. It sent a wave of chills down her spine, renewing the passion that simmered in her womb. "Would you have me hinder your own pleasure by spilling my seed prematurely? What sort of witch are you, Catriona Graham, that you can so easily make a man renowned for his stone heart, lose control so easily?"

She did not like the accusing tone in his voice. It smacked of arrogance. But the antipathy that had instantly reared its head went up in smoke as soon as he slid a hand down between her belly and the bed, and found her hardened pearl.

Catriona gasped and rooted for the blanket until she had it clamped between her teeth. Fire raced through her blood when he increased the pressure on her knot. Close, she was so very, utterly, maddeningly close to the edge of paradise...

But ecstasy, she suddenly determined, would only be hers when this man deemed it so. And that manner of male control wielded over her, making her helpless and at his mercy, only made her want him more.

"Ah, mmm...a witch," she groaned, her voice muffled, "who must get relief—*now*! Please, I beg of ye, John, please have mercy upon me."

"Oh, Catriona..." Words were not enough to express the ferocity of his need. He withdrew, penetrated, withdrew again. With each forceful entry, he shoved her further across the bed until her head hung over the edge, then her breasts.

Ah, to be filled by cock once again! It had been so very long. But no amount of celibacy could have prepared her for the sensations that bombarded her at this carnal moment. John's hot breaths increased in intensity, the panting and deep moans thundering in her ears. Her head spun with the heady scent of sex and frantic arousal. Sweat coated flesh, his melding into hers, hers into his. The slickness of skin glided over skin sending her body into a pleasant shudder of ecstasy. Heavy fire licked at her womb, making her mouth water and her wet pussy tighten around his enormous shaft.

No doubt about it, John had been forthcoming in claiming that he would do much more than please her. Already she welcomed the madness he had promised her, already she felt herself spiraling out of her normal boundaries of control. Duncan's penis had not been nearly this large, and she briefly wondered how she had ever been able to derive any pleasure at all from his small cock.

Aye, John reached depths that had not ever been traversed in her marriage, that had never before been touched. He pounded into her with relentless, animal force until she plunged over the edge of the bed, her hands slapping the wooden floor. John's hands followed, his arms flanking hers, but their lower bodies remained joined upon the edge of the bed.

"Oh. *Oh*, my God!" Catriona had never experienced such naughtiness. The angle of his cock inside her drove her into a crazed frenzy. Using the strength of her arms, she pushed up and against him. Her hair fell in a dark curtain around her face and she watched as it swirled and swished with each pounding. Sweat dribbled off John's chest and down her back, down into the hairline at her nape. The fire in the hearth seemed to spark and flame higher, while the musky scent of her own juices mixed with that of smoke and man became stronger, more addicting.

She could not get her legs spread far enough, or her ass up to an adequate height to sate her urges. All she wished for was his thick erection to spear her straight to her throat, to scratch that itch and bring her relief.

Her wish catapulted into reality, into the most explosive orgasm she had ever experienced. It hit her with the force of lightning, the power of thunder. She cried out at the same moment he did. Her body twitched. Catriona moaned out a long, unintelligible song as the fire torched her center and spread to her very toes and fingertips. Together they convulsed as one, their twined, sweaty bodies tumbling to the floor in a heap of spent muscles.

Breathing gradually returned to normal. Catriona lay there with her back to him, her knee raised, watching over her shoulder as the firelight danced upon the sharp, handsome angles of his face. His erection, now half hard, was so long it still partially remained within her passage even though they were no longer pressed groin-to-ass. His eyes were closed. With the half-smile curving the full lips, he appeared to be the epitome of a sleeping cat who had just slurped down his prey. One large paw spread possessively over her hip. The whole incident, the entire breathtaking picture he made, caused regret to flourish in her chest.

This would be the last time, she vowed silently. She needed to move on, to reach permanent safety. To never allow herself to be tempted by this sorcerer again.

*Ah, but he tempted ye beyond the devil's power, did not he, Catriona? Such a magnificent lover! But 'twould not be wise to become involved with some arrogant thief who would put yer life in constant danger one moment and cast ye out the next. Eh, God help ye, fool — ye* harlot! *Ye should never have given yerself up so easily to this caddish bandit!*

A knock sounded at the door.

"Who goes there?" John asked, rising to locate his braies.

"'Tis Falcon and Salena."

Catriona noted how John's eyes lit with surprise and warmth. "What the devil? I was not expecting you so soon."

"May we enter?" came the deep voice from the other side of the door. "I prefer not to speak through the thick wood of this blasted portal."

John chuckled, securing his garment. "Nay, I have a...guest within my chamber. We will meet you down in the dining hall shortly. Nelda has prepared the evening meal." He turned to Catriona and said in a low voice, "Get dressed. I would like you to meet my friends, as well as get some nourishment before you fly the coop."

She drew the sheet up and clutched it to her breast, dread and regret at what she had just done weighing heavy on her heart. "I do not wish to meet yer friends — or anyone else, for that matter. I must be on me way."

"You'll not be on your way, milady, not yet. You'll be staying here for the time being, and you'll be putting some victuals between those luscious lips of yours." He drew on the jerkin over his bare, wide chest without bothering to don a shirt. The strong, chiseled build and bulging muscles revealed beneath the strips of leather made her pulse flutter.

With a concerted effort, she focused on his handsome face. But she realized her mistake too late. The roguish good looks made her heart race with excitement. But resentment flourished there as well, resentment that he could affect her senses with such ease. She spoke through clamped teeth, focusing on her mission. "Ye cannot tell me what to do!"

He smiled, an expression designed to calm her, though instead it stoked the desire simmering in her abdomen. "'Tis all right, princess. You are free to go whenever you like. But I prefer you rested and fed first. And I request that you spend some time acquainting yourself with my special guests."

She shot to her feet, dragging the sheet with her. "I have survived these past weeks for days on end with little food. And I will continue to do so in order to be on me way."

He sauntered forward, his eyes never leaving hers. When he approached, she caught the faint aroma of his unique muskiness twined with her own scent. Something about it, about the warmth his huge body enveloped her with, made her knees go weak. In pathetic defense, she clutched the sheet, raising it until her fist nestled beneath her jaw. She could detect the determination in his gaze, in his wide stance and in the tautness of the muscles as he folded his arms across his chest.

"You will eat before you walk out my door, my love, or by God, I will chain you to the table until you have eaten an entire roast duck."

She gasped. "Ye would not do such a thing!"

He smiled, but not one flash of tenderness reached his eyes. "Try me."

"Oh..." She stomped a bare foot for lack of a sufficient retort.

"Here, upon the bench I've placed some clean male garments for you. Get dressed...or shall I do it for you?" He arched a brow. His pupils dilated, lending the blue of his eyes a roguish gleam that sent delicious shivers up her spine.

"Nae."

"Nay, you will not get dressed, or nay, I will not do it for you?"

"Both."

"Very well." He gripped her arm and bent, snatching up the shirt and braies. Backing her into the bed, he forced her onto the mattress so that she lost her balance. The sheet fell away. His gaze flashed to her breasts like a snap of lightning, sending a jolt of paralyzing fire to her loins.

"Nae..." She shook her head and scooted out of reach—almost.

He had his huge hand clamped around her ankle before she could scramble to the opposite side of the bed. "Oh, aye," he warned, yanking so hard, she feared her bone would break.

In a split second, she found herself naked and lying flat beneath his clothed body. The sensation of the heavy leather of his jerkin dragging over her nipples made her groan. The nubs ached, plummeting a whoosh of heat into her groin. Her pussy throbbed, and with humiliation, she felt a warm trickle of juice between her legs.

His mouth swooped down on hers, soft yet potent. She braced herself for the devastating invasion of his tongue, but it did not come. Instead, he held her face between his hands and kissed her with a tenderness that shocked her. Her body relaxed and the sorcerer swept her up into his wicked magic. Her toes curled, her hands fisted at her sides. Unable to resist, she wrapped her arms around his torso and sighed into his mouth, loving the wet, silky feel of his lips upon hers.

"Cat," he whispered against her mouth. "Please do not fight me. I beg of you to don the clothes and come below stairs with me. I simply wish to put some nourishment into your lovely body."

Her stomach chose that very moment to betray her with a growl.

"See? Even your body speaks to me of hunger."

Her face warmed. "Oh, all right. But then I must depart."

He grinned and smacked his lips against hers. "Good." Rising, he added, "I cannot wait for you to meet Falcon and Salena."

She sat up and located the clean garments where John had deposited them just before overpowering her. Her heart still fluttered as she replayed it in her mind. Hands trembling, she slid into the shirt and braies then sat to pull on her boots.

"Yer friends, who are they?"

John started for the door just as she stood and snatched up her cloak. "You'll find out soon enough. Hurry. I do not like keeping them waiting."

She followed him down a long corridor, her stomach fluttering with nerves. What if this Falcon were an acquaintance of the Scots king or someone in his court? Lord help her, but she could not take the chance. Her eyes darted around in search of an escape route. But she had dawdled too long. John turned and took her hand in his, its big, warm expanse closing around her cold hand.

"Do not even think of it, my dove. Come. You will dine with us, then we shall see about preparing you for your departure."

"It must be tonight."

"Mmm," he nodded, casting her a sidelong glance that defied his previous words of assurance that she would be free to go. "We shall see…"

At his evasive comment, she nearly stumbled, her legs trembling. We shall see? What exactly did that mean? Aye, Catriona knew she would soon find out. Nerves ate away at her stomach as he led her down a wide sweeping staircase and into the company of his friends. But were these friends truly foes determined to burn her to her death?

As she pondered that concern, they entered the great hall. The soaring ceiling drew her gaze, along with the open hearth in the center, and a raised dais set with a long fixed-top elm table and chairs. The room was empty, save for a woman setting up a side table with various foodstuff, including fresh-baked bread, wine and cheeses. The scrumptious aroma of roast fowl and stew wafted across the space to tempt Catriona. Her stomach clenched and the hunger pains intensified. It seemed all worries over her current dilemma dissipated and were replaced by her body's urge for nourishment.

She glanced up at John. "It smells heavenly. Thank ye for insisting I dine with ye."

"You are most welcome. Come." He led her to the table and pulled out a chair. "Please, be seated."

The gesture warmed her soul in a most touching manner. She sat, though she forced herself to throw up a wall. It would not do to fall into this wizard's trap of seduction and charm. *Catriona, ye would do well to remember this mon, with all his allure and fascinatin' aura, was truly nothin' more than a dangerous sorcerer.*

"I beg to differ with you, milady." The voice came from behind her near a door she assumed would lead to the solar above or into the kitchen. She screeched and twisted around, satisfying her curiosity to see who had intruded upon her thoughts. Her heart suddenly leaped up to choke her. One of the king's sentinels come to haul her back to Scotland, perhaps? Had John trapped her?

Despite the possibilities of danger coiling around in her brain, her mouth fell open, her derrière remained anchored to the chair. She could not help but scan the striking man, from the fair long locks, to the strong build clad in jerkin and braies, to the shin-high leather riding buskins upon his powerful legs and feet.

She drew in a long breath of air. Eyes to match the green spring meadows of her Scottish Lowlands swept her seated form before coming to rest upon her stunned gaze. Catriona grappled for the edge of the table and managed to scoot far enough away to rise.

"John, ye'll be tellin' me this verra instant... Who—who *is* this mon?" she demanded out of the corner of her mouth, never taking her eyes from the stranger.

John chuckled, leaning forward in his seat to pat her arm. "Not to fear, Catriona. 'Tis only Robin Hood."

"R-Robin Hood? Not to fear, ye say?" She did not even wait for John's affirmation. Leaping to her feet, Catriona shuffled away from the chair and staggered back until her spine pressed into the cold stone wall. Oh, how she longed for a chamber pot. Yes, with the sudden nausea crashing through her stomach, and this blond giant—a bloody thief and executioner!—standing before her, she would definitely be in need of that blessed waste pot.

Robin Hood, Prince of Thieves, murderer, plunderer, wily bandit. And like a bloody whore, she had given her body up to one of his cohorts! Queasiness roiled through her gut. Catriona stumbled to a far corner and fell to her knees wondering how she had so easily forgotten John's criminal status. She hugged her midriff as the fear and regret forced her to dry-heave the emptiness from her hungering stomach.

# Chapter Three

## ℘

Following an intimidating evening of supping with John, Robin Hood—or rather Falcon Montague—and his beautiful wife Salena, John had suggested Catriona bathe in the underground hot spring in the bowels of his home before departing. Now sated with a full belly, she luxuriated in the steaming water, and had found herself yet again tempted by the sinful lifestyle John thrust her into.

"I do not wish to discuss this barbaric topic any longer." Her nerves had somewhat calmed after meeting the infamous bandit, but the current topic of conversation had her ears perked and her heart thudding out of control. But in spite of her crisp tone and opposition, Catriona's entire body went limp in the heavenly hot water.

"The direction of the conversation—and the fact that the handsome couple had taken it upon themselves to join her and John in the pool—had Catriona feeling as if she had stumbled upon one of those rumored hedonistic, Greek bath parties from centuries past.

"Barbaric?" Falcon returned with an amused tone as he sat upon the rocky ledge with his legs dangling into the steaming water. "What, milady, could be so barbaric about seeking pleasures of unfathomable intensity—and *tripling* or perhaps *quadrupling* your pleasure, at that?"

Catriona did not know who this emerald-eyed rogue thought he was, or what he intended to accomplish, but she would not give in to this madness!

"I tell ye, I will not engage in...relations with *three* other people!" *Ah, but just sayin' it makes me burn with both curiosity and wanton need!* She sighed inwardly at the direction of her shocking thoughts. *What sort of carnal black magic, pray tell, did I happen upon that fateful hour when me path crossed that of John Lawton's?*

"Mmm, just what I thought…" Falcon said cryptically, his eyes never leaving Catriona's.

"Falcon," Salena scolded as she floated naked atop the water, her flawless body glazed with a wet sheen. "Do not invade the lady's privacy."

He gasped theatrically, his large hand slapping that thick chest of his. "Me? Invade one's privacy? Nay!" Falcon leaped into the water with a splash and worked his way toward his wife. "Not once in my immortal life, my sweet, loving wife, have I done such a rude thing."

Immortal? That brought Catriona around. She stared at Robin Hood and knew he did not jest. So he too, was a sorcerer?

Salena splashed and waved her arms until she stood up, the water lapping around her full breasts and ribs. She lifted a well-manicured hand and ticked off her fingers one at a time as she appeared to remember events foregone. Her gaze rose thoughtfully and fixed on the wooden beams crisscrossing over the stone ceiling of the cave. She smiled thinly, her blue eyes finally lowering to present Falcon with a level stare.

"Call me daft but, as I recall—mmm, nearly three score years past—you did just that to me, oh wily fox I call husband."

Falcon grinned wolfishly and yanked her into his arms.

"What? Eh, please, I cannot take these riddles any longer," Catriona choked out as she trudged across the pool, her arms folded over her chest to hide her nudity. *And I cannot deal with the temptin' wickedness of bathin' naked with others!*

"Salena speaks of Falcon's ability to read minds…such as yours, for instance," John offered, stirring the water nonchalantly around his nude torso.

Catriona stopped dead in the pool, mere feet from the edge, from escape. She whirled on John. "Beg *pardon?*"

From his place within Salena's embrace, Falcon cleared a sudden frog from his throat. He rested his chin upon Salena's head and fluttered one hand in the water. Through the random clouds of steam rising from the water's surface, she watched Falcon's gaze drop nervously, avoiding Catriona's blazing eyes.

"I—uh…I do apologize, milady. 'Twon't happen again."

Awe and mortification choked her. It was true! The man could read minds—had, in fact, read *hers*! Just like herself, just like John, it seemed Falcon possessed a form of supernatural abilities, as well. And why did that surprise her so? She had already accepted the truth of John's powers. But another? Aye, as amazing as it seemed, it appeared to be so. Now that she thought of it, she could clearly recall Falcon's words earlier this eve when he had entered the great hall. As bizarre as it seemed, he had apparently "overheard" her thoughts.

*I beg to differ with you, milady.* Falcon's words, which she had not comprehended at the time, had directly followed her own thoughts regarding her cynical feelings on John, on him being nothing more than a dangerous sorcerer. Oh, but it boiled her blood to learn that this man Falcon had read her mind—invaded her privacy—and known both sides of her struggling emotions where John was concerned!

"I cannot bear these—these *intrusions* and this-this utter *lunacy* any longer." Catriona spun back and pushed her way through the vaporous water. She started to climb from the depths of the pool, but turned and growled, "All of ye, I demand that ye turn yer backs at once. I tell ye, ye will not be seein' the likes of me backside in the nude, not without a fight on yer hands."

Not one of them, not even John, protested. All three of them, including Lady Salena, turned their backs. Certain they all continued to obey, she finally rose from the pool. Catriona took the underwater stairs two at a time until she reached the stack of linens set within a carved-out shelf in the rock wall. Swirling the cloth around her, she gasped when the voice called to her.

*"Catriona, Catriona. Please, milady, I beseech you to allow me to come through."*

Catriona's eyes snapped upward. Her body swayed and quaked as her vision blurred. A female spirit called to her making her groan. Of all the bloody times for her to be summoned from the other side!

"Aye, but I ask, who are ye?" she demanded, clutching the linen towel to her chest.

"Cat, what is it?"

She heard John's concerned tone behind her, but waved a hand to him. "Shh."

*"I am called Maid Marian. For an eternity I have searched for a medium to reach my love, Robin. Please, will you inform him I am here?"*

Catriona slowly turned around. Her gaze found Falcon's. "Do ye ken a maid by the name of Marian?"

He blinked, a stunned look flashing in his eyes. "Aye. But she is long dead."

Salena gasped but did not say a word.

"She has just called to me. She wishes to inform ye she is here."

"What?" Falcon swam to the pool's edge and looked up at Catriona, his mouth hanging open. "Marian is here?"

"Hush one moment." Catriona held up a finger. "She speaks again."

*"Tell him I am proud of all he has accomplished as a vigilante. Convey to him as well that I approve of his beautiful wife and am so delighted that he has found happiness and no longer mourns my passing. Up until Salena came into his life, I had been in constant misery for him."*

"Oh, God help me," Catriona groaned. "Do I have to?"

*"Please?"*

Catriona sighed, feeling more and more uncomfortable standing in front of three virtual strangers in naught but a towel while held hostage by an insistent spirit. "She says she is proud of all ye have accomplished." Her gaze moved to Salena's stricken face, and emotions of joy for Salena came to the forefront. Emotions Catriona did not expect to feel. "And she declares she approves of yer beautiful wife. She is happy, Falcon, that ye no longer mourn her passin' and have found happiness."

Falcon spun toward John even as Salena began to sob in delighted relief on her husband's behalf. "Is this a cruel joke, man?"

John shrugged. "Is it a joke that you can read minds, my friend? Nay, 'tis not. By the same token, I believe this demonstration is not in jest either. But if skepticism plagues you, why not focus on Catriona's thoughts and see what comes of it? See if you can disprove her claim..."

"Oh, bloody hell." Catriona moaned her displeasure at this untimely interruption to her escape.

"'Tis fine!" Marian exclaimed in elation. "I welcome the opportunity to speak with him."

"May I?"

She found it laughable that he asked her permission for something he had apparently done without asking before now. "Farthing stars above, I do not believe I have a choice, now, do I?"

"Cat, you do have the option to deny him," John supplied, hauling his naked body up to sit on the far ledge. "At least this time you do," he said arching his brow in warning at Falcon. "Does she not, my good man?"

"Aye, I will bend to her desires and honor her privacy if she so wishes. But if 'tis true and is all right with my wife, I would very much like the opportunity to speak with Maid Marian."

"So be it," Catriona said on a sigh, waving a hand. "Do yer thing, mon, but get on with it, would ye?"

"Salena?" Falcon turned to his wife, a look of hope in his eyes.

"Oh yes, my love, yes!" She nodded vigorously. "I am pleased you have been given this occasion to speak with her. I accept your lasting love for one another and would never deny you this."

"Thank you, my dove." Falcon choked it out with an edge of warmth and adoring love to his voice. He turned back to Catriona and narrowed his gaze on her. She watched as his eyes sparked with something powerful.

"Marian?" Though he spoke aloud, Falcon's voice entered her thoughts as well, right within that space in her brain where she always spoke with the dead. The prospect of it had her gasping in surprise. Never before had living people been able to enter the cusp in her mind that allowed her to see into the afterlife. But then again, Falcon was a wizard by all accounts.

"Falcon!"

"Gods alive, 'tis true. Our Catriona does speak to the dead," Falcon replied in astonishment.

"Aye, ye lout, now get on with it. I have a journey to embark on verra soon."

"Falcon, I have attempted to find a conduit to reach you ever since my passing. My soul cannot rest in peace unless given the opportunity to tell you the one thing I never could…"

"I cannot see you. Please, Catriona, can you allow me to see Marian?"

"'Tisn't me decision. Marian?"

"Nay, my handsome bandit, nay. 'Tis best this way. You now have an adoring, beautiful wife who loves you beyond measure…as do I. Yes, I have loved you always, Falcon. I know I never conveyed that sentiment clearly enough to you, but 'tis high time I did. And I thank your Gypsy lady here, for allowing me the juncture to do so."

"Yer so welcome. Now can we get on with it? Och! I must go."

"Ah, Marian." Falcon ignored Catriona's plea. "I never doubted your love. Aye, 'tis true you did not speak it. But I knew that to be an attempt to further protect me and my Merry Men from the Sheriff of Nottingham. In spite of that, your love was very apparent."

Catriona heard the soft release of sobs and her heart went out to this dead woman.

"Thank you, my love, thank you. You cannot know the anguish and frustration of needing to express this to you, of not knowing if you had been aware of my love and then being unable to find a way to inform you. Now, 'tis time for me to finally pass to heaven. Go forth, be happy and love your wife beyond even that which we had."

He turned so that his gaze raked his naked wife, her body slick with steam. "Aye, I will. That I will."

"Goodbye, my wily thief Robin Hood. I love you."

"Farewell, my love." He said it with half an ear on Catriona's conveyed thoughts, his attention now on Salena.

It was at that moment Catriona experienced the lessening of both Falcon and Marian's energy. Relief flooded her body and she relaxed, glad to be rid of her burden.

*"Thank you, Catriona,"* Marian murmured, as her voice faded into nothingness.

"Yeer most welcome. Go forth and rest in peace."

Falcon only had eyes for Salena. He spun in the water and swam across the distance to her. Catriona caught one last glimpse of him as he took his beloved wife in his arms and kissed her with thorough, robust passion.

In all his nude glory, John hauled himself up and started around the edge of the pool toward Catriona. Avoiding his hot stare, she fled up the curved stone stairs, running as fast as her damp feet could safely take her.

Behind her, she heard John's expletive and a rustle of water followed by Salena's stern tone. "No, John. I'll go. This is clearly a time for a woman-to-woman conversation."

\* \* \* \* \*

*Like the bloody fires of hell,* "woman-to-woman" Catriona thought as she hurriedly donned her male clothes. This was utterly absurd. She had heard of such hedonistic behavior whispered among her Gypsy friends and rumored to be practiced at court. This joining with multiple partners was complete lunacy — but never had even her own free people engaged in such bizarre practices! It was unheard of — as far as she knew. Mostly fairytales told to stir the blood and entertain.

But not within the circle of Robin Hood and his Merry Men, apparently.

A knock sounded upon the thick oak door.

"Begone with ye, I say, whoever the bloody hell ye are."

The door swung slowly open leaving Lady Salena's small but curvaceous frame outlined by the portal. She stood proud, her chin up, dressed once again in her man's braies, jerkin and stark-white linen shirt. Her deep auburn hair hung loose in long waves over her shoulders and down her back. The shirt had been left unfastened to well below her impressive cleavage. A fascinating blue stone — a stone that matched her pure blue eyes to exactness — nestled in the valley of her creamy-toned chest.

Catriona felt a stirring of — what? Envy? She supposed that was what it was for the woman's voluptuous body could not be denied. Certainly John too had noticed…

"Do ye not have ears?" Catriona stuffed her own man's shirt into her braies. "I said begone with ye."

"Aye, I have ears," Salena agreed, stepping into the room. "And I have eyes, as well."

"And what, may I ask, is *that* supposed to mean?"

"John."

"Ah, so the lady can see John. I applaud yer good eyesight," Catriona sneered as she turned her back and fastened her codpiece around her waist.

"No need to spread your claws, Cat. I am but here to help you, to hopefully make you see things it seems you cannot see for yourself."

"Ha!" Catriona whirled and faced this breathtaking woman with what she hoped was her best look of hatred. "Ye do not ken what ye babble about, do ye? I have seen things nae one else sees! I *see* the dead, Lord God help me!"

"I am very aware of that, based on what just occurred belowground. And I do, by the bye, thank you from the bottom of my heart for giving Falcon the gift of speaking with his long-dead lover. Though I know he loves me more than his immortal life itself, he has expressed concern in the past that his relationship with Marian was never quite resolved. He did not know what the unresolved issue was, but it was a vague sensation of something needing to be settled. Apparently, he could sense her angst but did not know how to solve the mystery. You have helped to make him the happiest, most fulfilled man in the world. And for that, we both thank you."

"Eh, I did not do it of me own good heart. I did it out of nothin' more than curiosity."

Salena took another step closer, her hands folded primly before her. "You heard a plea from a trapped soul and did what you had to do. Curious or not, to me, the deed speaks for itself."

"Speaks? Aye, ye can say that again. I hear their bloody tormented voices too much to count the many times. Their longin' to be back on the other side with their beloved ones tears at me heart and frustrates me to no end."

"Of course it does." Salena's voice came out in a soothing English accent that made Catriona think of a royal, gracious princess. "'Tis a sign of a caring woman."

"Ye think so? Then why have ye accused me of not bein' able to see things for meself? Eh? Well, ye might be interested to hear," she barreled on, not waiting for a reply, "despite the king's crusade to have me head on a platter, I only see and do what I have to to mend the healin' between the livin' and the dead." Her voice rose almost hysterically. But instead of losing control, she snorted, swirling her cloak around her body. "I *see* it all, but *I* choose when to act upon it! Do ye ken what I say?"

"I...I'm sorry," Salena murmured on a sigh, stepping up close enough to press a warm palm to Catriona's cheek. The woman was small compared to Catriona. She had to look down into the delicate, upturned face, into those mesmerizing, ocean-blue eyes. It somehow calmed her, made her anger dwindle to a mere simmer, as if she had had a tirade in front of an innocent child and knew she had made a fool of herself.

Salena went on, her hand caressing Catriona's cheek. Reluctantly, Catriona allowed the warmth to permeate her skin and calm her nerves—just for a bit.

"Please, you must understand John—nor any of us—means you no harm 'tall, in any way. Did he not save your life twice? You must understand I speak of what I see as only a woman can comprehend, as a woman who has been in your very position before. So you see, 'tis those magnetic looks he casts your way...and you him, that I speak of."

Catriona jerked her face from the tender palm. "Aye, he saved me life on two separate occasions, that I'll be ownin' up to. But still, it does not mean—I do not ken what ye speak of. 'Tis ridiculous."

She did not know why, but Catriona allowed Salena to hook her arm around her waist and lead her to the settee positioned at the foot of the bed. They sat together, and Salena angled toward Catriona so that their knees touched. Strangely, it gave her a kindred and tender feeling, despite the antipathy that had burst within her chest moments ago. As a result, she welcomed the calm and took a deep breath, silently vowing to hear this woman out.

"You will understand soon enough, Catriona. You will, I assure you. But for now, may I ask that you please stay?"

She shook her head vehemently. "Nae. I must be on me way to—"

"You are safe here, I promise you. They do not know where you are. Do you not know already of John's strengths? He has informed us of how he whisked you here by his amazing *invisilation* powers a score of miles away from the location where you last were preyed upon—and nearly killed—by the Scottish king's men. You are much safer here within the English border and behind the impenetrable walls of John's keep than wondering afoot in the wild where at any moment, they could happen upon you."

"Aye...his powers. I do thank him for healin' me and givin' me me life back, to be sure. But..."

Salena's eyes sparkled as her mouth curved into a sunny smile. "Ah, then 'tis settled! You will stay with us for as long as you like."

Her flippant words struck a note of caution with Catriona. "Us?"

"Mmm, us...did not John explain we visit now and then because of his need for energy derived from intimacy?"

"Aye—well, nae, but—"

A single auburn eyebrow dipped in thought. "Uh, mayhap I should leave this up to our John to explain."

*Our* John? "Nae! Don't ye dare leave me in suspense. I demand to ken this instant what ye allude to."

"Very well," Salena sighed. "You see, he needs the energy, as does Falcon, though John's powers deplete much sooner. I have—we have—been assisting him with that replenishment on occasion for decades now."

"Ye what?"

"Shh, hear me out. Falcon, too, needs to be refueled on a regular basis, but as soul-brother to John, they derive huge, longer-sustaining powers when they couple as a trio."

"Ye…come to think on it, this is what Falcon jested about down in the hot spring. So they wish to make it a quad instead—to multiply their powers further?"

"Ah, now the lady's got it!" Salena grinned, but her face swam before Catriona's vision. Despite the shock her ears were even now struggling to decipher, Catriona's clitoris began to throb. It was mortifying, it was taboo at its worst…it was making her heart race. Wetness poured out onto the crotch of her braies.

"Why, that is—nae. How can ye claim to love Falcon if—"

Something almost volatile snapped in Salena's eyes. "I love Falcon with all of my heart, soul, body and life. 'Tis why I urged him to speak with Marian, and why I gift him with infrequent triads with John. I love John dearly too, but not in the same way I love my husband. 'Tis the least I can do to gift both men I love with life-sustaining energy. Oh, yes, I most likely derive more pleasure out of our couplings than the two of them do combined. But nonetheless, I do it first and foremost out of love for my husband, and secondly, out of loyalty, friendship, and yes, a different sort of love and affection for John."

"Nae…" She pressed her hands to her ears. To hear the intimate details of this bizarre triangle made Catriona feel much like an outsider. Was that jealousy eating away at her innards? Nae! How preposterous. Oh, but the carnal, forbidden pictures that kept flashing in her mind seemed to taunt her, made her womb feel heavy and achingly warm.

"I know you have feelings for him."

The outrageous words had Catriona snapping her gaze up in shock. She leapt to her feet. "I will not say it again. Nae!"

Salena reached for her hand, drew it to her own face and rubbed Catriona's palm against her silky cheek. "Oh, aye. 'Tis as plain as the birth of spring. But you do not have to surrender your heart so soon. Your body...'tis another matter altogether. Please, just think about it very carefully, Catriona. It would be a most special gift of powers we could give them both. Besides..."

She planted a feather-soft kiss on Catriona's palm. It made her breath shudder, her pulse leap.

"Besides? Besides what, melady?" Though she longed to keep her hand within Salena's, she ripped it out, ignoring the cold disappointment it left within her breast. "Please do go on, and then begone with ye."

Salena rose. She stood before Catriona, her ripe breasts nearly pressing just under the swell of Catriona's bosom. Catriona inhaled catching the floral, rosy scent of woman. Strangely so, it pleased her, made her relax a small measure and be glad to once again have female companionship, just as she had had with the Gypsy caravan as far back as she could recall.

Oh, but this bit of respite would not last long. Soon, she would be on her way, leaving behind all this calm and tempting grandeur. It made her stomach lurch with dread, but she pushed it aside, drawing on her bravery and fortitude of the past months. She pushed it aside too, in order to address the delicate matter at hand.

"You see, I have never experienced the touch of another woman," Salena said almost cheerily, despite Catriona's harsh tone. "Now that I am secure in my relationship with Falcon—especially with Marian resolved—I can only guess that it would add positively to the mix, and most likely increase his stores of power more so than with the three of us. I cannot promise to instinctively know how to bring you pleasure. But I beg of you, do this thing—just once, at least—for John, the man I adore, for the one I am certain you will grow to love. And most importantly to me, at least, I want my husband to go on living into eternity—as I do John. I want John to be happy with a woman for once. And I think you just might be the one to do that for him."

Her head spun making her collapse back onto the settee out of necessity. This forward woman had a knack for barreling right into things, going from one shocking topic to the next. It was all Catriona could do to keep up with her.

Confused, Catriona croaked, "And how, I ask, do ye ken I would be 'the' one?"

"Why, your eyes, of course..." Salena whispered, bending to press a gentle kiss to Catriona's stunned mouth. "They match John's *Scorpian*—exactly. And the *Scorpian*, it dictates John's future just as the *Centaurus*—" she lifted the medallion from its place nestled within her cleavage, "ruled Falcon's."

With that, Salena turned and sashayed from the room, leaving Catriona's head in a whirl, her lips tingling and her pussy embarrassingly soaked. And uppermost, she wondered...just what in bloody hell was a *Scorpian*?

# Chapter Four

 හ

"A blizzard currently rages outside the keep. You will stay until it passes — and that is an order."

Despite Salena's enticing request to consider remaining longer and joining in their taboo practices, Catriona had bundled herself up to depart. She was just opening John's chamber door when he appeared before her outlined by the portal, his massive width and height filling its space.

With her hand on the ornate knob, she shot back, "I answer to no one. And no one orders me about."

He stepped inside bearing down on her in such a foreboding manner she had no choice but to let go of the doorknob. Too late she realized it to be a mistake, for he kicked the door shut behind him caging her in.

"Nae! Ye stay away from me, ye bloody brute." Catriona backed two steps to his every one. But to her distress, she soon learned his stride proved far longer than her own.

His hand snaked out and fastened around her forearm. In a flash, he slammed her against his chest, his arms closing around her like heavy chains in a dungeon. The wild scent of anger, and yes, arousal, filled her nostrils.

Those eyes frosted over. "You will stay."

"Oh, ye are infuriating!" She attempted to lift her fists to pound them on his chest, but her arms were held captive by his iron-hard grip. The movement only succeeded in making her wiggle against his rising erection. Despite the lust that washed through her, she spat, "I hate you."

A single dark eyebrow winged up. "You hate the gallant gentleman who has done naught but bring you pleasure and save your life—and twice at that?"

Very well. Perhaps she did not hate him, but she despised the sardonic tone in his voice.

"I-I...ye be no gentlemon if ye insist on holdin' me against me will." She twisted with a grunt. "Unhand me at once!"

He ducked his head and buried his face in the crook of her neck, inhaling her scent. The resonance of his blissful sigh made her eyelids go limp sending a wave of delicious gooseflesh down her body.

"Please, my Cat, do not force me to lock you in my chamber. Stay with me just this eve. On the morrow, we shall see about getting you on your way."

She moaned when he drew her earlobe into his mouth and flicked his tongue over it. Shimmering flames scattered through her system, settling in her womb so that she could swear she heard the sizzle of hot coals showering her moist pussy.

"Time," she panted, gripping the braies at his hips in defense. As if to mock her feeble resistance, a log shifted in the hearth across the room. *An omen, perhaps, of what would come?* she wondered. "I do not have time to dally. The bastards hunt me as we speak, and will not give up until they have me tied to the stake and burnin' in hell."

"Aye, is it not obvious I should be somewhat aware of that, given the fact I rescued you from those very bastards? So you wish to go to London then?" he asked, grinding her pelvis against his hard cock while his free hand rose to entangle the hair at the back of her head. He nipped a trail across her jaw, and drew her up so her lips brushed his.

Gods alive, she had truly met her match with this wizard! With one touch, one smoldering look, he could have her pussy wet and throbbing, and her knees buckling beneath her trembling body. "Mmm, ye know I do." She slid her hands up and hooked them behind his neck.

"Then there is a simple solution. I shall *invisilate* you to your destination—as I did to get you here in the first place—as soon as the storm passes. It will take but a few moments to get you there, much, much faster than by foot."

"*Invisilate* me, ye say?"

"Aye, *invisilate*. Now shush, my stunning young maiden, and let us enjoy this time we have together."

"But—"

He hitched her up so she straddled him. Turning, he stumbled forward. Her back slammed against the heavy wood door making her suck in a breath. Catriona recovered quickly when she realized she liked being overpowered and ravished. The urgency to depart John's manor now a vague need, she locked her ankles behind him. In the process, his thick shaft crashed into her clothed vee. Somewhere in the whirl of things, she understood what he offered her. It was the perfect solution. She could remain here and dabble a bit more in his seductions, and yet still be far ahead of the king's army and lost in the crowd by the time they arrived in London through the conduit of his black magical powers. A heavy weight lifted off her shoulders and left her in a state of manic glee. Aye, his offer was far too alluring for her to pass up.

"Ye are a wicked wizard, ye are, enticing me so." She dragged her lips over his as she spoke, and let out a quivering whimper when he cupped her breast through the shirt. "Ye tempt me beyond reason."

He rolled her taut nipple between his fingers, the rough fabric of her shirt increasing the sparks he lavished upon her. "Does that mean you will stay?"

"Do I have a choice? Not only have ye threatened to lock me up, but ye've cast yer spell of seduction upon me once again. How can a lady resist such debauchery?"

"If you felt half the passion I do at the moment, you would know there is not resistance, but complete surrender." Levering her against the door, he slid his hands around to her ass. His fingers brushed her cunt through the fabric of her braies. "Ah, my gorgeous Gypsy, you are so wet, your honey soaks through your britches as we speak."

Her heart thundered, pumping the lust through her system at an overwhelming rate. She had to get these cumbersome clothes off. Now. "Let me down," she panted, squirming against him. "Let me down now so I can get the bloody britches off."

"No need," he rasped, raining kisses over her cheek and down her neck, making her shiver in anticipation. She had gone mad, Lord help her, but all she wanted, all she needed, was his big cock filling her cunt.

Even as he continued his devastating seduction, he swept one hand from her shoulder to her leg. "Garments begone." Prickles of heat arced through her entire body, like hot water splashing her from head to toe. She gasped when her clothing disappeared and cool air assaulted her flesh. But it did not take long for the heat of his big body to envelop her. And when his naked manhood pressed against her clit making her groan, she realized his garb had also vanished.

"John..." She threw her head back. It thunked into the door. But the stars she now saw swimming before her vision, had burst forth when he entered her. "Oh yes."

His huge rod filled her to the depths of insanity. She constricted her legs around his waist and held tight to his neck. Waves of sharp pleasure rushed through her pussy making her hot slickness tighten about his shaft. Her breasts bounced and her nipples brushed his when he drew back and thrust his penis into her once again. His hard pebbles scraped her rigid areolas, and Catriona thought she had never felt a more naughty sensation in her life.

"Ah, so tight, so moist." His shoulder muscles flexed beneath her forearms as he palmed her backside, kneading her ass cheeks, stretching her anus open. Warm, wet lips hovered at the corner of her mouth, his hot breath fanning her cheek as he spoke in that deep, raspy tone. She pulled back, stared into his handsome face and saw the look of a man on the brink of losing control. It thrilled and empowered her beyond description, validating her womanhood.

"What you do to me, Cat. You make me daft, utterly mad with passion, like no other woman ever has in my long, immortal life."

Catriona sucked in a breath. The exclusivity of his words shocked her, and coupled with the glow in his eyes it made her pulse leap in alarm. In them, she saw a deep affection that gave her pause, affection much more intense than any she had ever experienced in her past. She did not know how to label it, but despite her unease, her own emotions mirrored his. It boggled her mind and distracted her from the pleasure at hand.

*Nae, whatever this is, ye cannot allow it, Catriona. Take yer pleasure and move on. Ye must always remember yer life is at stake here and ye cannot involve others.*

"Shh," she whispered. "Do not speak. Just take me, John. Fuck me hard and fast, and make me never forget ye and yer lovely cock."

"Oh, God, Cat, how can any man deny that sweet, sinful request?" His mouth slammed into hers. She tasted ale and blistering, urgent need as she feasted on the silky fullness of his lips. Their tongues mated, dueled, as did their sexes. John drove into her with demanding force, his big cock fulfilling yearnings she never knew could exist. Her bare back crashed and scraped the door, but she didn't care. It gave her the support and strength she needed to fight back, to give back. She levered her hips up and down, taking him in, releasing him, but never letting him go. Frissons of fire raced behind every move and motion. It built like the flames in the hearth, power catching to fuel, fire combusting into an inferno. He rocked harder, faster, just as she had requested. His fingers dug into the globes of her ass as he developed a rhythm, lifting, slamming, lifting, slamming. Each propulsion increased the momentum so that her pussy became engulfed in a constant firing of pleasure.

Bliss loomed near. Her cunt juices poured out onto his groin. He grunted, his body suddenly stiffening. Catriona cried out, the climax rippling through her at the very moment he closed his mouth over her nipple.

"John…" Pleasure such as she had never felt before, took her senses by surprise and made her toes curl. Hot and cold, sweet and bitter, so many things bombarded her she almost knew a need to escape the overwhelming bliss.

But he was not through with her. He sucked the sensitive nub into his mouth and plunged his cock one last time into her canal. Her upper body slammed against the door. His body spasmed, and she let out another wave of moans when his hot seed filled her womb.

Outside the keep, the winds howled as the snowstorm blew in. In the aftermath, they clung to one another, the only sounds in the room that of the crackling of the fire and their ragged breathing. She ignored the soreness in her back and instead focused on the erotic sensation of their perspiring, warm bodies melded together, of his cock still buried to the depths of her soul. Even now as they stirred, silently caressing one another, she could smell the aroma of their passion. She marveled that it could all bring raging need for him back to the surface once again. Yet the entire encounter, every stimulated sense, brought reality crashing back.

Regret moved in, hovering over her like a dark storm cloud. She could stay here like this forever, but forever was only for immortals and souls on the other side. No matter if she chose to stay indefinitely or nay, time would eventually tear her from him. And Catriona never wished to go through the pain of departure again.

Bloody hell, when would the snowstorm end?

\* \* \* \* \*

Indeed, the storm lasted for days on end. So with John stubbornly refusing to transport her until the weather had calmed, she was forced to remain in his hedonistic abode.

Since arriving at John's estate, Catriona had been afforded the luxury of a bed for the first time in months. Salena had loaned her a gown that first night, the soft fabric snug but heavenly against her skin. It had been a long time since she had indulged in such blissful yet simple sensations as that of a true bed and clothing meant only for slumber. Unable to resist the respite and comfort of having an actual roof over her head that protected her from the raging blizzard, she had agreed to stay for just one more day...which had led into another day, and then another. She now had been here at John's estate for nearly a week.

Salena's bold, hedonistic suggestions, as well as Catriona's fears of further intimacy and avoidance of heartbreak where John was concerned, had her that first night insisting John show her to the safety of her own assigned quarters. His bed had been heaven that day he had made wild love to her, but she would not be tempted by it or expected to occupy it without her own space to flee to if need be. Exhausted, she had not protested when he had ushered her into the suite that adjoined his chambers by one thick oak door void of a lock. A tray of cheese and wine had welcomed her, yet another example that his continued hospitality showed no boundaries. As the storm dictated, one night had led into two, two into three, in which she made a concerted effort to remain in her chambers to avoid the three of them while refueling herself for her departure. Holed up in her suite the entire time, she allowed only one maid by the name of Adda to come and go in order to provide her with meals and assist in her toilette and bathing. She spent many late-night hours curled in bed watching John's shadow move across the light below the adjoining door, listening to the bandit prowl about. Burning for his touch.

Fully sated once again this night, clean, dry, fragrant down cushioned her and tumbled her into instant, blessed slumber. She did not want to think of returning to the harrowing days of her recent past, of hunger, cold, fear and constant running. Instead, she burrowed into her temporary warm hiding place, away from that cruel outside world, away from the powerful and vengeful Scots king, James VI.

And she dreamed...

"Me Catriona, how could ye have betrayed me so?"

She turned slowly, as if her body had been swallowed up in a deep puddle of mud. That voice...was it Duncan's? Ever since his horrid burning ordered by the king for witchcraft, she had not once been able to reach him on the other side. It had always troubled her, always made her feel so lost and alienated from him. Why was it that she could reach almost any spirit without difficulty, but she had not been able to contact her very own dead husband?

"Duncan? Is that ye?" Hope bloomed in her chest.

"Aye, 'tis yer husband." He stood there, the fire that surrounded him imposed over an endless darkness at his back. The orange, angry flames outlined his thin frame making him appear even more slender than she recalled.

Something troubled her instantaneously. What was it... Oh, God, forgive her, but why did her heart not leap at first sight of him as it always had before his passing?

"But...but why? Why have ye finally come to me, and in a dream, no less? Ye ken verra well, 'tis not me normal mode of contact with the dead."

Though the fire rose higher behind him, a biting chill blew in, ruffling her nightshift. She hugged herself in search of warmth and stared at him, still puzzled by her vague indifference to him. Aye, he was a handsome man with his jaw-length auburn waves and eyes of gold that had always stirred her sex. But now, now at this moment, it was not so in the least. It perplexed her that her legs did not carry her to him, that her heart did not leap with passion.

"Stupid wench, would ye rather be in contact with *him*?"

His accusing, hateful tone made sudden fear crawl through her abdomen. "Him? D-Duncan...do not speak in such riddles, and with yer voice so verra obnoxious in tone. I ask ye, husband, are ye not glad to see me?"

He moved toward her, his black cloak swaying as he sauntered across the darkness. She could see now that his eyes had turned into flames, so very much like the devil's abode. Catriona gasped, trying desperately to retreat, but she could not move. Her legs seemed to be anchored in place, and would not obey her mind's commands to run. She could almost hear her pulse pounding all around her, mocking her with her own apprehension. The flesh over her bones felt cold, oh-so-very cold, even though fire raged around her.

*'Tis only a dream, Catriona. 'Tis only a dream.* She recited it to herself over and over, but it did not seem to lessen the rising trepidation that sliced through her abdomen.

He floated closer until his eyes were a finger's thickness from hers. Terror tore at her chest and a scream lodged in her throat. She could smell acrid ash, burnt flesh, his horrid breath. Despite the foul odors engulfing her, Catriona pulled on every breath fighting to get air into her lungs. If she did not get away soon, she feared she would faint right into his vile arms.

"Ah, me wife—nae, *whore*—what is the matter? Do not like what ye see?"

"Duncan, please do not do this to..." The skin upon his normally handsome face began to rot before her very eyes. Wiggling, squirming maggots suddenly feasted on his pale flesh. She watched, horrified, stunned and unable to move, as the critters went to work and devoured his skin, leaving behind nothing but skull and cracked bone. A sickening new odor, one of festering filth and vomitus, filled her nostrils making her stomach toss and turn with nausea.

His wicked laughter echoed around her. Flames continued to burn in his eyes, yet now, the fire hung suspended behind the open sockets surrounded by grayish-white bone. She looked down to see his dark clothing had faded away and the maggots continued their quest down his entire body.

"Duncan, nae! Please, do not laugh so wickedly. 'Tis awful, 'tis horrid! Are ye hurtin'?"

He did not speak again. Instead, his skeleton stood there trembling as his heinous guffaws turned to a sort of cackling, evil tune. It grated on her nerves, made her long to run as far from this reprehensible man as possible. Why was he haunting her this way? Why? And how had she ever loved such a detestable man?

*'Tis just a dream, Catriona. This is not Duncan's spirit, it is not — cannot be — the spirit of yer dead husband!*

"Catriona."

The deep, raspy voice made her jolt. It sounded so pleasant, so kind in comparison to Duncan's hateful tone. She wiped the tears and turned her back on her dead husband. "Who…who goes there, I say?"

An elderly man clad in a dark brown monk's robe appeared at her right. His silver beard hung long and thick. It glowed in stark contrast against the garment. He glided nearer and she arched her eyebrows at first sight of his eyes. White. Save for the black dilated pupils in the center, his eyes were entirely snow-white, set in the wrinkled mass of his leathery face. One gnarled hand clutched a tall crystal staff. She noted the unusual gold medallion dangling long from his neck, so lengthy it hung below the pointed beard.

Where had she seen it before? The stone, so green, so…pure and beautiful. Familiarity nagged at her intuition.

Catriona angled more to face the stranger. "Who…ye'll be tellin' me at once, I say, who are ye, sir?"

"Mmm, throughout the long ages, they have practically christened me as Lorcan. By all means, feel free to do the same, Miss Catriona."

"Lorcan? Why, I do believe John spoke of ye a time or two. Come to think on it, as I recall," she chuckled melodiously, the horror of past minutes now forgotten in the dream phase, "he referred to ye as a daft old wizard."

The darkness surrounding them swirled with flames, though a distant brightness haloed the edges, like the sun clamoring to get through a storm cloud.

Lorcan scowled, his bushy silver eyebrows bunching together as one. "Eh, that blasted John Lawton." He lifted the staff and stirred the flames, sending up plumes of smoke. "Arrogant bore, would you not agree, Catriona?"

She could not help but let out a resounding giggle. "Aye, ye may certainly say that again, wizard. Now, how is it that ye ken me name?"

He lifted the medallion from his chest, his bony hand trembling. "Because of this, and because I have seen into the future. My foresight...well, 'tisn't always correct, but I have a very strong sense here. You—you *have* to be his chosen one. It must be so. It must!"

"Chosen one?" Her voice rose high and disbelieving. "Seein' into the future, ye say? That is utterly insane! I must admit, I tend to agree with John's characterization of ye."

Thunder rumbled in the distance. The winds stirred and she caught the subtle scent of anger mixed with ancient flesh and some odd mixture of ale and ginger. Lorcan lifted his staff and drove it into the blackened space beside his foot. The ground shook beneath Catriona's feet. She gasped, attempting to aright herself before falling.

"Bah! Do you not see into the past yourself, in a sense, into the afterlife?"

"Aye...aye, that I do, sir." Under her breath, she mumbled, "But how could ye ken of somethin' that is none of yer affair? And why is it that ye cannot just speak forthright and dispense with the bloody riddles?"

Lorcan threw the rod down and crossed his arms over his thin chest. "None of my affair? Hmph! So, if you are gifted enough to see into the *afterlife*, then what, lass, could be so daft about an old wizard seeing into the *future*? Opposites and yet alike, wouldn't *ye* say? Why, I ask, being as gifted as you are, do you not just see it as truth rather than riddle?"

Catriona didn't know if it was the fuzziness of the dream state she found herself in, or the old man's twisted form of logic, but she seemed to be growing weaker, groggier and extremely confused. It made it very difficult for her to reason out exactly what the sorcerer alluded to.

"Look, 'tis time for me to be on me way, far, far from the king and his men, just as I have been tellin' yer friend John. So please, if ye would be so kind as to excuse me..." She turned, but the twiglike fingers that clamped around her upper arm possessed far more strength than she had assumed would be the case. Forced to look into the white, almost marbled eyes, she shivered in revulsion.

"I insist ye unhand me, sir."

"Be forewarned, I will return to you when the time is right."

"Nae, I-I appreciate yer...generosity, but nae, I shall forego that invitation, if ye please."

Lorcan grinned, revealing a row of surprisingly white teeth. "'Tis not your choice, milady." He threw his head back, cackling, and clutched the medallion once again. "'Tis that of destiny's choice. Oh, aye. No doubt about it now that I see for myself." He held up the amulet and studied it. His gaze moved back and forth between the unusual green stone and Catriona's eyes. "Mmm, like it or not, seems to be out of your hands, lass."

"Nae...I must be on me way, I tell ye! I *must*! Neither ye nor John nor King James' entire bloody army will keep me from me quest."

His image began to fade into the inferno. Though she could no longer see him, she could still hear his voice, hear him begin to chant as the fires around her intensified.

"Oh, Catriona Graham of Scotland afar, to avoid the bloodshed of hatred and war. Your gift and your heart, your pillar of life, 'twill lead to an eternity as your chosen one's wife."

"I'll be repeatin' it one last time—*nae*! Old man, do not go without explainin' such a twisted riddle! Old man, I—"

She heard the ragged breathing before she saw him. Heart thudding in her chest, she turned to see Duncan stalking her once again. His eyes were still ablaze with hateful flames.

"Nae..." She backed away, but her foot slipped off the edge of darkness.

"Ye will burn, witch...just as I did," Duncan said, a satisfied smile curving his lips.

"Duncan, how can ye treat me so? Oh, 'tis a dream. 'Tis a nightmare, Catriona," she murmured to herself as she receded further into nothingness.

But the next step sent her tumbling right into the flames. Searing, unbearable pain engulfed her body. She could feel the sensation of her back pressed against a wooden stake, her body being roped to its rough length. The smell of her own singed flesh and hair made her nauseous.

"Burn, witch, burn..." Whose voice was that? The king's? Lorcan's? Duncan's? Or perhaps John's? Lord help her, but she could no longer tell one from the other. Catriona could not think, could not breathe, but she managed to force out one final scream.

John sat upright at the bloodcurdling cry. "Holy gods of eternity!" He flipped the blankets aside and leapt naked from the cozy warmth of his bed. It did not take but a second to locate his braies and don them. John strode across the room and yanked open the door that adjoined his chamber to hers.

He could see that dawn had arrived, by the pink and orange shimmer lighting the pane of the window just beyond the bed. Disappointment stabbed at him, for he knew that meant the end of the snowstorm and thus, her inevitable departure.

She lay on her back on the down mattress, her arms and legs outlined by the morning's light as she flailed and kicked at the covers. By the waning firelight that remained in the chamber, he could see the look of utter terror on her face each time she turned toward him. Her beauty had been tearstained and marred by emotion. It made him long to cleanse those rosy cheeks with soothing kisses. His heart ached and twisted in his chest even as he stalked to her with the long, impatient steps of a man on a dogged mission.

"Catriona." He eased a hip onto the bed next to her. His hands stilled her arms with a gentle grip. John shook her just enough to bring her to awareness.

"Nae!" She screamed it out in agony. The loose, blue-black tresses streamed over John's hands, the fine texture reminiscent of unruly spun silk. Inhaling, he caught a soft floral scent—perhaps loaned by Salena? He noted the clear complexion had returned to its normal tawny tone, the diminishing firelight dancing in obscure shadows and light upon its perfection.

"I do not wish to burn. Please, Duncan, why are ye doin' this to me—*nae!*"

The man's name on her lips made John's teeth grind. Concurrently, the thought of her burning at the stake, and the terror she must be dreaming of, sent his heart into a painful, thudding protest. "Catriona. You must awaken. 'Tis all right. You are not burning. You are safe here with me in my home."

Her eyes fluttered open, two dew-dappled, drowsy emeralds set within the beauty of her heart-shaped face. He tore his mesmerized stare from those confused orbs and glanced lower at the movement of her chest. It rose and fell in short, panicked spurts of breath affording him a delectable glimpse of full, smooth breast. Eternal gods, how it stirred his blood, made him fight the urge to take her this very minute with swift, unbridled passion!

"J-John?"

Ah, to hear his name upon her lips in such a relieved, almost endearing tone. To see the light of relief in her eyes when the fog of the nightmare gave way to the reality of his face. And to feel her damp hands now clutch at his upper arms with inconsolable need... Every bit of it, every tiny nuance did something to his soul's core, made him feel all warm and glowing inside.

"Aye, 'tis me, your lifesaving thief."

"Oh, John!"

She threw herself into his arms. It had been too many days since last he had enjoyed her charms and held her body to his. He gasped inwardly, stiffening at the abrupt display of impassioned emotion. The scent of warm, pliant woman filled his lungs and drifted into his blood like a potent, intoxicating ale. For one long moment, he held his arms out in indecision, but she clung to him with desperation, molding her body to his as they both sat upon the bed. Unable to resist one second longer, he closed his eyes on a sigh and gathered her snug to his chest.

"Shh, shh," he rasped, combing his fingers into the thickness of her hair as he rocked her body with his. "You are fine now, my Cat, just fine."

She shook her head, her voice muffled by the flesh of his chest. "Oh, if 'twere but true!"

He pulled her back and stared into the eyes of a frightened lass. In that moment, his soul melted into hers, it seemed. John fought the urge to crush his mouth to hers, to claim her as his once and for all. He had never in all of his days been so utterly bewitched by a woman's beauty. And oh, how it unnerved him to the point of madness!

"'Tis true, Gypsy. I vow to keep you safe for as long as you will allow it."

She snapped her jaw shut and gaped disbelieving at him. "B-but, ye do not even ken me."

He could not help but slide his hands up so that his palms cupped her face. John dragged one thumb across her full bottom lip and watched, pleased when her eyes went limpid and she turned her face into his palm.

"True, I know you but intimately, though I wish to know every nuance of you, as well, everything that makes these alluring eyes of yours narrow in anger or twinkle with glee. And everything in between."

He leaned in and pressed his lips to hers, drinking of her flavor, tantalized by the silky wetness of them. A sharp quickening in his belly sent a rush of blood to his cock. He felt his balls draw up in anticipation of release.

"But—"

He shook his head to halt her dissent. "Nay, I do not require to know a person inside and out in order to protect them from evil. Ah, but I have just made the determination that I would, nonetheless, like to become familiar with all of you…if you would but give me the opportunity."

"Och, mon. 'Twas but a dream ye cannot protect me from. But this dream, this horrible nightmare…it seemed so verra, verra real." She shuddered and he drew her closer.

"'Tis all right now, love." He paused for a moment rubbing her arms with his hands as curiosity burned in his brain. He longed to call Falcon in to spy upon her thoughts, but that would only serve to chase her further away. "Care to talk about the dream?"

"I… Nae, 'tis done and well gone, thank the stars of the blessed dead." She glanced away, her wide gaze drifting to the window's display of the dawning of a clear day. A quaver hovered beneath the surface of her voice. "John, I cannot dally much longer. Ye…ye do not understand. I dare not—"

"Mmm," he murmured, ignoring her reference to departure. "I love the way your voice is released between your lips all breathless and husky with emotion when you speak. Your brogue enchants and holds me spellbound, like a symphony of harps. Frankly, Catriona Graham, I'm captivated by every little thing about you."

"John…"

"Shh."

Unable to resist—and he supposed as a tactic to distract her from the lovely weather outdoors—he slid one hand down into the neckline of her gown, slow, deliberate, until his palm became filled by her breast. She gasped and the nipple sprang to life against the pad of his finger. His free arm glided downward. As it made its maddeningly slow trek, he caressed her shoulder, her spine, each plane and angle of her waist, until he had her held firm to his side.

She groaned, her head tipping back so that her long tresses brushed his knuckles. "And I find meself spellbound by a sorcerer." She hissed it out with a note of half-reluctant passion, half-injured pride. The ambiguity only endeared him more to her.

Inhaling deeply, he drew in a lungful of her sleepy aroma. "Oh, my Cat." He captured her mouth with his, and pressed her back into the bed so that his lower body covered hers. John tasted paradise, his tongue sweeping and probing into the sweet sea between her lips. She breathed in, breathed out, her chest falling and rising into the hand he continued to explore her breast with.

Greedy now, she combed her fingers into his hair, drawing him down tightly against her. She devoured his mouth as he did hers. *God of eternity, have mercy!* John's pulse beat erratically. His cock throbbed. He ground the hardened mass into her warm thigh, reaching for relief that would not come.

Already, revitalization poured into him just from her amorous kiss. But John had to get closer. He needed more—he needed it all. Dragging the gown up with one firm stroke, he found what he sought. The soft curls gave way to the wet petals of her pussy. She whimpered into his mouth when he stroked the swollen clitoris. His movements were slight and fluttery in the beginning, just enough to make her want more, to send her upward toward a pinnacle she could not return from. Catriona's body writhed beneath him, and she cried out and bucked when he finally buried his middle finger into her sticky passage.

"Oh!" She tore her mouth from his. Her voice came out in a succession of short rasps. "Ye…oh, please. John, I-I do so want ye again."

"Want 'tis a strange thing, is it not, Catriona?" His teeth nipped first her jaw, then the silken flesh of her neck. His finger moved in and out, coated with her white cream, warmed by her passion. As he spoke, he shifted and slid the gown up further with his other hand, all the way until the peaks and slopes of her chest were bared for his perusal. Both nipples sat atop the mounds like glistening jewels. He hungered for them, longed to taste every inch of her flesh both outside and in. So he did.

*Lord of immortals, she tastes salty and sweet, like a decadent French tart!*

"It can make you wild," he went on, seducing in whispers. "That burning want can make you do things you would never have thought to do before now…"

"Aye," she murmured. "Aye."

He inserted another finger, joining it with the first. She moaned, thrashing her head from side to side as he closed his mouth over one tight knot. "Like making love with me…"

"Mmm-hmm." She nodded her head vigorously, arching her back when he rammed a third finger into her pussy. His teeth clamped playfully onto the areola.

John held up her breast, slathering its roundness with his tongue. "Like allowing others to watch as I bring you to climax?"

"Mmm, I...oh, ye're such a wicked mon." Her sweet song came out on a shudder. "Ever since I opened me eyes to find yer healin' hand at me breast... Ah, ye tempt me beyond distraction."

Her words pleased him more than he could say. Aye, he yearned to be her *only* tempter, and a large part of him wanted her completely to himself. But Salena had suggested something to him and Falcon recently. Her notions of magnifying their powers twofold taunted John, teased him to utter lunacy. Images of the four of them entwined in lovemaking embraces burned in his mind like smoldering coals in the hearth. He knew what benefits and pleasures it would bring them all, including Catriona, even if she did not comprehend it just yet.

John had heard the door open and click shut shortly after he had gathered Catriona into his arms to soothe her fears. There had been no need to see for himself who had entered her chambers. He had known without a doubt Falcon had come to apprise himself of the situation, to make certain the screams had not been due to danger within John's quarters. It was merely a part of their bond and caring, a facet of their brotherhood that went unsaid between them.

This very instant, Falcon and Salena both watched. John knew it with a sharp instinct without even glancing over his shoulder. Falcon's cock would be stiff within his braies, his upper body bare after bolting from bed. Salena's pussy would be hot and slick with desire as she watched John make love to Catriona. Her nipples would be pressed like ripe berries against the thin fabric of her low-necked nightgown, the

*Centaurus* dangling between her full breasts. And she would be watching with a sparkle of approval in her aqua eyes.

Aye, the prim woman of years past, long since turned wanton. It had all been Salena's suggestion, a foursome rather than their usual trio. She fervently hoped making love with two women at once would bring about twice as much immortal energy than John and Falcon normally gained with one woman. Salena's eternal life, it had seemed, had evolved into such a feverish love for her husband and a fondness for John, that she had become a near crusader in the cause to keep them both powered.

"You speak of temptation, my vixen?" He shoved her arms above her head and drew the gown up, exposing her lush body for all to see. John dragged it over her face but he left the sleeves on her arms. Winding the bulk of the garment around her forearms, he bound her in place.

She whimpered, her emerald eyes glazing with lust. "More. I yearn for more. Please, remove yer braies."

"Look at you now. A shrine of seduction," he accused, ignoring her plea.

"More…"

"Oh, I promise you," he warned, "you will get more, *much* more." Holding her arms in place with one hand, he took the other and shoved the braies down over his hips, kicking them off.

"Hmm, promises from a thief. Ah, if only he would just deliver and cease snatchin' me verra breath from me lungs," she rasped, her flared hips bucking against his thigh.

Such true womanly passion, such inborn seduction! If his cock got any harder, it would burst. Just knowing Falcon and Salena watched her response to his touch brought John to a whole new pinnacle of pleasure. And he wanted Catriona to feel the same rush in her loins, wanted to be certain of her desire as she learned of the hedonistic turn of events.

He wedged his way between her legs and aligned his rod with her cunt. "Turn your head, my love, there toward the portal. I want you to see what your beauty and fire have caused, what promises you seek."

Her dark eyebrows dipped in confusion. She licked her lips making him thirst for their dew. Slowly, she rolled her head to the side. John entered her at the precise moment her gaze became fixed on Salena and Falcon. Catriona gasped followed by a strangled moan of ecstasy.

Slick. Oh-so slick and tight! Being a tall, slender woman, her body had no problem accommodating his length. The girth of him was all but choked by her snug pussy. He nearly spilled his seed right then and there.

"T-this is not happenin'. They...they are watchin' us." Lustful fascination edged her voice. Her hips began to move. He felt her inner walls spasm around his penis. John looked down at her, her arms secured above her head by the haphazard wind of her gown. He could see one eye narrowed with yearning as she kept her head turned toward the door. A wild, animal-like gleam shone from its depth, as if she were a surrendering mare being ridden by the king stallion. He studied her regal profile, the small, straight nose, the lips swollen by his kisses. And, oh, that body!

"What are they doing, Catriona?" He bent and tasted of the dusky slope of her neck. "Describe it to me."

"Mmm, John, oh, John...that feels so verra good—and 'tis so wicked what they are doin'."

He drew back and rammed into her, his breath escaping in a ragged wisp, just as hers did. "I beg of you, tell me, what wicked things do you see, Cat?"

"She is half naked...ah, such a beautiful little body. He has her...bent o'er the back of the chair. And, oh, John, h-his..."

"His what?" John demanded. That sexy Scottish burr only added to the allure of her. It made him crazy to hear the husky, accented edge, to feel its robust stroke in his ears. Beyond control now, he yanked the gown from her arms and gathered her up so she could cling to him. Unable to bear it any longer, he swung his gaze to see Falcon nude, forgotten braies down around his ankles. His powerful body tensed and glistened by the firelight as he stroked himself in and out of Salena's hole. She was bent over a wing chair near the fire, her gown shoved up over her hips, the round swell of her ass jiggling with each pounding thrust.

"God help me, but his shaft looks so verra huge and...nice."

John let out a groan. He was almost there. But he had to hear it from her mouth first. "Will you do it? Will you make love with me—and them at the same time?"

She cupped his face in her hands. Pressing her mouth to his, she murmured, "Aye. For ye, to see if 'twill give ye the massive powers Salena theorizes it may. Please ken, me thief of hearts, only for ye do I agree to yer hedonistic request. To supply ye with that much needed energy just this once before I depart."

Despite the mention of her impending departure, glee slammed into him at the exact moment the orgasm escalated. "Thank you, my Cat." He thrust in and out of her slickness, loving the scent of her sex, her soft flesh against his chest, her warmth. John took her mouth in a gentle, insistent kiss, drinking of her wild flavor. And he knew he had fallen in love with a witch when her muffled cry of ecstasy filled his mouth at the exact moment Salena and Falcon groaned out their pleasure.

John's body spasmed with the energy he took from Catriona. He spilled his seed into her womb and collapsed in a heap of centuries-old relief.

# Chapter Five

ॐ

"Who is this Duncan chap?" He lay on his side facing her, his head propped upon a fist. With his free hand, he trailed a finger over her hipbone, skimmed her silky waist. Across the room, Salena and Falcon silently prepared to slip from the room.

Catriona's gaze darted lethal and sharp to snare him with an incredulous look. She slapped his hands away and drew a blanket across her nakedness. "Where did ye hear that name?"

He stared agog at her, briefly stunned by her brusque reaction. "From your own lips, Catriona. You dreamed of this Duncan. You called out his name in sleep with utmost fear in your voice."

"Nae!"

"Oh, aye." He leaned closer, determined now to get to the bottom of this abrupt change in mood. John reached across her and planted one hand on the bed. The heat from the swell of her hip warmed him to the very bone. "Now I inquire one last time, who is he?"

"He is Duncan McNicol of the clan Nicol," Falcon said as he pulled up his braies and fastened them. He strode around the chair and across to the adjacent sofa, Salena on his tail. "Of the clan she no longer pays homage to."

Catriona's sharp, indrawn breath preceded her scathing words. "Ye bastard! How dare ye invade me mind? How *dare* ye?" She scrambled up and away from John, huddling alongside the mahogany headboard, the blanket drawn tight beneath her chin.

"My apologies, milady," Falcon said with conviction as he sank into the overstuffed settee before the fire. "But with your life in extreme danger, I find it necessary."

Salena curled onto Falcon's lap and wrapped her arms around his neck. Normally, the move would have roused John's libido, but there appeared to be a pressing matter at hand before pleasure could be sought once again.

"Catriona, none of us — particularly John — are here to hurt you." Salena gave a gentle smile, one that had her eyes twinkling with emotion. Her long burnished locks flowed over her bosom. "You must believe that. Obviously, your troubles over this Duncan plague you even in sleep, otherwise, we would not have been awakened by your screams of terror this eve."

Teardrops glittered in the corners of Catriona's eyes making John's heart ache. He started to reach for her, but halted at her words. "'Tis none of yer affair. *Any* of ye."

John eased back, hardening his expression. "We shall see about that."

"Mayhap ye are daft and a wee bit too arrogant for yer own good," she snapped back on a sniffle.

He could not help but clench his jaw. "Nay, simply practical...and finally accepting of Lorcan's visions."

"Lorcan! Why is it this old wizard seems to have a place in everyone's life?" she spat.

"Everyone?" Falcon put in from across the room. His voice held a trace of curiosity laced with a knowing assurance, despite the single, questioning word.

Salena slid a glance of womanly insight from John to her husband. She unfolded herself from Falcon's lap and glided toward the bed, her gaze fixed on Catriona. Salena's full breasts bounced as she walked, the pink nipples straining against the thin fabric of her gown. "We all must know...have you seen Lorcan?" Salena asked of Catriona.

The low firelight leaped and flickered behind Salena as she sashayed nearer. John could see the luscious swell of curves outlined by the orange shimmer of light, the contours of her labia silhouetted by the glow of the fire behind her. Tenderness, gratitude and a sort of awe for this special woman welled up inside him. Nay, he would never be able to love her as Falcon did, but there was a bond there, one between all three of them, that would now have to be expanded to include Catriona. Oh, she would not be accepting it anytime soon, but if he could not convince Catriona she belonged here, fate would play its usual role and do it for him. And it seemed Lorcan had already been playing his part in seeing to the future as well.

As John watched Salena move closer, he thought of Catriona's lush body. With the exception of Salena's, it had fit his large girth like no other woman in history had—nay, even more precise than Salena's. Catriona had not feared his big size upon sight, or experienced the usual pain and tenderness during lovemaking that usually sent women fleeing for the hills. That alone, *Scorpian* and fate aside, proved to be enough to seal his future with her. Her gift of love to him would come with time...if it had not already. If the surprisingly strong surge of love he felt for her did prove to be reciprocated, this Duncan fellow—whoever the bloody hell he was—would have to be eradicated from her mind.

"Gentlemen..." Salena sat next to Catriona, nudging John aside. He rose grudgingly and stood at the bedside. In spite of their partially clad bodies, Salena gathered Catriona in her arms, ignoring Cat's rigid response. Only the linen sheet Catriona coveted and Salena's sheer gown stood between them. "Please leave us this instant."

"Nay." John shifted his stance and started to sit.

Salena halted him. She reached out and curled her hand into his, her eyes angling up at him with stern affection. "We must ease her into this, John. Go now—and take Falcon with you. Imbibe in a tankard or two of ale, then return in but an hour's time."

"Ale so early in the morn'?" Falcon chimed in, sidling up beside John.

Salena waved a hand. "Ah, then break your fast. Just go. It—she—will be fine."

"Do not speak of me as if I am a child forgotten in the next room."

"I am sorry," Salena said gently, her jovial gaze shifting to Catriona as she patted her arm. "It is sometimes necessary to converse with thick-skulled men in such a fashion."

Catriona suppressed a short giggle that warmed John's heart. Mayhap he should step out for a bit and see what magic Salena could work on the stubborn woman? Between the three of them, they should be able to get to the bottom of this Duncan character whom seemed to have plagued Catriona's past.

Falcon slapped John companionably on the back. "I believe my wily wife has spoken. Come along, my good man. Let us go and see what mischief we can stir up with the cook while the ladies converse in that female manner…which a man will never comprehend."

Salena snorted. "Be off with you both!"

John nodded. "As you wish." His wavering gaze took in the sight of the two women sitting adjacent to one another on the bed, Salena's left arm draped over Catriona's bare shoulders. It did something to his insides, made his stomach tighten with both desire and an unexpected bit of jealousy. It was irrational, he knew, but nonetheless, it made his body go taut with anxiety as he jammed on his braies and stepped from the room.

*What has this Scottish Gypsy done to me in such a short time?*

Falcon shut the door behind John and turned on the heel of his bare foot, his flaxen hair streaming down his naked back. He started down the corridor with a spring to his step. "I do believe I will break the fast with some ale, after all. Mayhap wash some ham and eggs down with it. Join me, brother?"

"You know, do you not? You read it in her mind," John accused as he fell into step beside Falcon.

Falcon raised a golden eyebrow and cast John a sidelong look as he descended the straight rear stairway leading down to the kitchen. "Hmm?"

"Goddamn it, Falcon, do not toy with me. Who is this Duncan fellow?"

"Ah, that."

"Ah, that," he mimicked sourly. "Falcon, I warn you—"

"Very well. He is Duncan McNicol. 'Tis her deceased husband of the Nicol clan I spoke of earlier. She is estranged from her in-laws and it seems has taken back her maiden name Graham in the process. But she does not know why they have cast her out in the aftermath of her husband's execution."

John set his jaw and followed Falcon below stairs. Guilty relief washed through him that this Duncan did not live, that he had proven to be her long-dead husband. So why did a strange sense of foreboding immediately replace the short-lived pacification in his gut?

* * * * *

"You spoke of Lorcan," Salena began, settling against the headboard at Catriona's right.

"Aye, he came to me in a dream."

"Hmm, he did but the same to me decades ago during the early, stormy days of my relationship with Falcon." She glanced at Catriona's bare cleavage peeping through the gap of the linen sheet. "But I see you do not wear the *Scorpian*. Did Lorcan not offer it to you in this dream?"

"The *Scorpian*?"

Salena nodded eagerly. "Aye, the medallion I mentioned to you days ago. In your dream, did he not wear the golden amulet adorned with the unusual emerald...just like your eyes?"

"Nae—aye, he wore the chain with the stone. But what would that have to do with me?"

Like her eyes? At the echoing thought, Catriona shivered. Yes, that was why the stone had seemed so familiar in her dream. It had been as if she had looked into a single duplicate orb of her own eyes.

"Because, 'tis my belief 'tis yours by fate's right, just as the *Centaurus* was mine. Yours used to seal your destiny as John's chosen one." Salena reached for her hand and weaved her fingers into Catriona's. At first, Catriona's instinct was to withdraw, but the tender gesture eased warm and soft into her system. It was enough to make her nearly overlook Salena's words. Instead, her ears perked and she twitched her gaze to the right.

"This cannot be. Ye have just used the exact words of those in me dream, those spoken by this Lorcan. 'John's chosen one' he had called me."

"Ah." Salena's mouth curved up ever-so slightly at the corners. "This does not surprise me."

Catriona came up on her knees, heedless of the sheet falling away from her nakedness. She looked down into Salena's lovely, startled face. "I tell ye, I cannot become anyone's wife!"

"Wife?" She said it more as a smug statement than as a genuine inquiry. "Do you recall me saying such?"

"Nae, but this Lorcan, he recited some ridiculous riddle, one that spoke of me gift and me heart leadin' to an eternity as me chosen one's wife. 'Tis utterly absurd! I've but kent John for one week's cycle, I tell ye. And this Lorcan...who is he— nae, *what* is he?"

Salena reached up and curved her palm over Catriona's cheek. She rose up on her knees, as well, and leaned closer, so close, Catriona caught the sweet floral scent of woman mixed with raw sex. It pleased her somehow, in spite of the topic. It made her feel calm and at ease on the one hand, yet excited and intrigued on the other.

Salena's eyes betrayed her excitement. They sparkled like two turquoise gems upon the Firth of Forth waters. "That settles it, then! There is no doubt in my mind John has finally found his intended. Why Lorcan chose to gift me with the *Centaurus* in my dream and yet withhold the *Scorpian* from you, I do not yet know." She giggled, clasping Catriona's hands into her own small ones. "But I do not care! 'Tis a moot point, and it shall work itself out in the end."

Catriona collapsed to the bed, drawing the pillow to her breasts. She squeezed its feather softness and stared into nothingness. "This is all happenin' so verra fast. I-I do not ken how to process it all."

"Shh, shh," Salena soothed, drawing Catriona into her embrace. The warm, soft skin, the sweet scent of rose wafting up from Salena's hair, it all rushed into Catriona's senses. It pleased her, made her nerves calm somewhat, but it proved to be the curve of breast pressed to her own that intrigued and sent her system into a strange gallop.

She recalled Salena's speculation on the possible compounding of John and Falcon's energy. Gifting them with two women at once rather than their usual one, according to Salena, might bring them untold quantities of energy. Catriona's thoughts scattered, bounced from one emotion to the next. Visions of Salena being ravished between the two handsome men made Catriona's heart flutter with a reluctant thrill. But it quickly turned to envy when she thought of John's massive cock entering the passage of this gorgeous woman.

The three of them obviously had something special together. It made Catriona feel like an outsider peering in through a forbidden window. Yet her wayward, wanton heart still yearned to experience their fascinating union, to taste of the titillating, taboo concept of multiple, inviolable companionship she had heard whispered in her band of Gypsies.

*What would it be like?* she wondered, even as her pussy throbbed with the possibility. To have two men at once—and one who had quickly gained a very special place in her heart. Ah, but both were so breathtakingly pleasing to the eye! To think they would be pleasuring her…and another woman at the same time. It boggled her mind knowing it was hers for the taking. And she somehow knew there would be nothing dirty or temporary about it. She had but to say aye to their earnest needs and ecstasy would be hers. Dare she?

"Catriona?" Salena gripped Catriona's shoulders and firmly held her away. "Are you all right?"

She blinked, her eyes coming back into focus to take in the face of an angel, a woman who she knew could become a true friend if she just allowed it. "I-I am fine."

Salena combed a hand through Catriona's hair making her shiver with delight. "You are sure?"

"Aye."

"We may take this as slowly as you wish…or not at all. 'Tis completely your choice. Both Falcon and John will respect your wishes."

Her choice. In some strange manner, those few words freed her from that one shred of indecision. Aye, it was her choice. They were not forcing or coercing her. She could flee this place if she so chose, or stay as long as she wished. She could refuse to participate in this experimental carnality proposed for John and Falcon's sake, or offer to gift them with a lover's energy to power their sorcery to a possible level not yet achieved.

"Hmm, 'tis me choice, ye say…"

"Oh, aye," Salena said with earnest, shaking Catriona gently. "There was a day many decades ago, before this…" She lifted the *Centaurus* from her breast turning it this way and that. Dawn had since broken sending shafts of orange light through the open window. The blue, cat's-eye-shaped stone glittered, nearly blinding Catriona with its brilliance.

"A day that I longed for choices," Salena went on, "only to realize Falcon had been giving me the option all along to say nay to his charms...and to John's. 'Twas merely my own prudishness, my ingrained morals and propriety's standards that held me back. Ah, and the most important fact that my betrothed awaited my return. But my quickly evolving love for Falcon during my captivity, and the respect and fondness for John and their brotherhood, made me realize I had it all for the taking, and that I was not meant to be with my betrothed." She grinned impishly. "Pray tell, what red-blooded woman would not want two gorgeous men fawning over her?"

*Indeed.* Catriona relaxed a small measure and pressed her palm to the back of Salena's right hand where it still clutched Catriona's upper arm. "Aye, I believe I am beginnin' to understand what ye mean."

Salena's mouth curved into a relieved smile. "Truly?"

"Truly."

"You do understand that I—we—would not be opening the bond of our triad to just anyone, do you not? In fact, in all our decades together, we have never invited another person to join us."

Catriona scooted across the bed and rose, dragging the sheet with her. "Aye, that I am beginnin' to comprehend, as well. I ken this is not taken lightly by the three of ye, that rather than as a shockin' insult, I should take this as an immense compliment. And I suppose I do."

Salena leapt to her feet. Her eyes glistened with unshed tears. "Then you will do this thing for Falcon and John?"

Catriona clutched the cloth to her chest and paused for just a moment, long enough to allow herself this one last chance to turn and flee. But her pussy pounded with a relentless curiosity and desire she could not resist any longer. "Nae."

Salena's expression fell into one of dejected disappointment. "Oh, well, then…"

"I'll be tellin' ye now, I am verra uneasy about this, but I do it for *John*. I fear I am fallin' in love with the arrogant thief. And since there seems to be a bond between him and the two of ye that I cannot or will not break, I concur."

Salena threw herself against Catriona's sheet-clad body. The feminine form molded to her, and that rosy aroma once again engulfed her. Catriona stiffened at first, but it did not take long for her to embrace the woman when she felt Salena quiver with emotion.

"Thank you. Thank you *so* very much, Catriona."

She felt petite, warm and soft in Catriona's arms. Faint waves of a strange desire fluttered deep in her womb. Though it did not stir her blood to the echelon John did, it was pleasing on a lesser level. Aye, she could do this, by Scots! She *would* do this. And she suspected she would be enjoying herself far more than she ever thought she would.

Catriona drew Salena away from her chest and looked down into her tearstained face. Something struck her at that moment, something that made her heart warm. Friendship. She had had many women acquaintances in the band of Gypsies she had grown up with. But none had melted her heart so swift and sure as the emotion that now clutched at her soul. It felt wondrous and heartwarming. It felt so very right.

"Nae." Normally a hard woman by necessity, Catriona could not believe her own eyes stung with sentiment. She sighed inwardly and smiled with sudden relief. "Thank *ye* for takin' me as friend, for trustin' me to engage in passion with ye and the only two men ye care about in this world. I am honored and wholly humbled. Now," she murmured, attempting to choke back the tears as she slid her hand down into Salena's, "let us go and seek out our men—and pleasure their souls with our powerful, feminine wiles. In the meantime, I am quite curious…what is this about a gentlemon betrothed and ye being held in captivity?"

\* \* \* \* \*

*You both must come below to the underground cave. It is of an urgent, dire matter. Please hurry! Love, Salena*

Salena had perched herself at the secretary's desk in the chambers she and Falcon always occupied while visiting John's keep. After relaying to Catriona the entire shocking tale of her kidnapping by Falcon, and her brother's sinister part in a plot to murder her, Salena scrawled the words onto parchment paper, and promptly returned the quill to the ink well.

"There. That should send them running to us like two knights rescuing their damsels of woe." She giggled. "Mayhap they will worry so acutely, John will even *invisilate* them to us."

Catriona's heart fluttered with the little plan Salena devised. Now that she had made the commitment to go through with this taboo affair, she could not contain herself. Catriona's clitoris throbbed in anticipation. She could barely withhold her juices as they threatened to spill from her pussy.

"Mayhap," Catriona echoed with an excited quiver to her voice. "But however 'tis they arrive, it must be soon before I faint."

Salena winked and rose from her seat. "Faint, you will, lovely Catriona, once you get a taste of our lovemaking." She paused as if she pondered her next words and chose them very carefully. "You do know you are the first woman—besides myself—that John has ever brought here to this home, do you not?"

The cryptic proclamation was enough in itself to make her heart still. "Nae, I did not have an inklin'. I...oh, dear."

Salena reached for Catriona's hand and squeezed it firmly. "Do not worry, love. This is a very good thing. Here, take this," she said as an afterthought, plucking a fur-lined cloak from a nearby peg and shoving it into Catriona's hands.

Salena reached for another for herself. "'Tis chilly where we are bound. Now, let us be on our way."

Stunned as she was, Catriona could do naught but nod and agree. She obediently took the cape and draped it over her arm.

They swept from Salena's chambers into the corridor, Catriona clad in her braies, linen man's shirt, jerkin and boots, and Salena in a lovely day dress of deep navy. Catriona watched as Salena's gaze fell upon a servant exiting John's suite with feather duster and dirty garments in hand.

"Althia!"

The plump brunette woman turned, her eyes widening. She deposited her load on a nearby settee and waddled toward them. "Mercy, 'tis Lady Montague! Welcome back to Sedgewick Castle, melady."

Salena glided up the hallway, smiling all the way as she pulled Catriona along with her. "Thank you, Althia. 'Tis good to be back. Where have you been this last week since our arrival?"

The woman waved a dismissive hand. "Eh, tendin' to me grandson, the little rascal. Master John gave me some time off."

"Good for you!" Salena peered through an open chamber door where housekeeping appeared to be in session. "You know, you always keep the house in such excellent order for our John. I am sure your talents were missed."

The woman bobbed her kerchiefed head. "Oh, aye, aye. Always for the master. He is such a good mon and well deservin' of bein' pampered. Ah, and I do thank ye for yer kind words, melady."

"It does not surprise me that you would take such good care of him. You are such a valued employee."

Althia grinned, revealing a toothless gap in one corner of her mouth. "And I teach me Edwina to honor our lord as much as I."

Salena tsked. "Ah, Edwina is but a babe."

Althia's mouth rounded as she shook her head. "Oh, nae. She be nearin' a good dozen years. Wee bit more than a bairn, that she be. And here I was thinkin' —oh, pardon me manners! Good day to ye, miss." She nodded with a quick curtsy to Catriona.

"Please, please," Catriona said hurriedly when she realized the woman honored her. She put out a halting hand. "I thank ye, but do not bother with formalities. There is nae need."

Althia gasped theatrically. "Ah, it warms me verra heart!" She layered her hands and pressed them over her ample chest. "A genuine Scottish lass in me presence."

Catriona mentally winced. Her stomach twisted into a regretful knot. How foolish of her to speak when she had instantly recognized the woman's accent! It would be to her advantage to remain as anonymous as possible. She did not trust King James' tactics or any of his soldiers in pursuit of "witches". Making herself known to anyone, especially a native Scot, might be tantamount to suicide.

Catriona managed a warm smile. Already caught, she did not wish to draw attention to herself or to insult the maid. "Aye, and I see by yer sweet brogue ye hail from one and the same," she said to Althia in Gaelic.

Althia nodded and returned her comment in their native tongue. "Mmm. Eastern Lowlands at Edinburgh, just off the lovely Firth of Forth. Once lived to the east of the grand Edinburgh Castle upon The Rock. Nae more for me, I tell ye. 'Tis right cold here, that 'tis, but—" she shivered, "I'll be takin' the south any day."

Catriona laughed, instantly taking a liking to the woman. She switched back to English. "I have yet to test the seasons, but I will be takin' yer warnin' to heart."

"Althia," Salena put in, obviously eager to get on with their plan. "May I ask that you go below stairs and see that Lord Montague receives this note?"

Althia reached for the sealed, folded message. "But of course, melady!"

"Thank you. You are a kind and valued friend." She angled to her left and hooked her arm into Catriona's. "Shall we be on our way, then, Catriona?"

"Aye, please." *Do get me as far from the Scotswoman as possible!*

"Althia," Salena nodded, dismissing the servant as she guided Catriona back the way they had come. To Catriona, she said under her breath, "I am privy to a back way to the caves below the manor."

"The caves, ye say?"

"Mmm, the hot springs where we all bathed that eve. 'Tis why we have these." She indicated the cloaks and donned hers. Catriona did the same. "This particular passageway 'tis a cold journey into the bowels of the manor."

"Ah, I see."

Salena guided her down another corridor, a different one from which John had taken her the previous trip below. They proceeded through a sitting room of sorts and on to a far door set in the corner. She pulled it open and revealed a darkened, hidden stairway. A faint, musty scent wafted up to invade Catriona's nostrils.

"Come." Salena lifted her skirts and descended into the darkness. "Close the door behind you. 'Twill be dark but an instant. Just hold to the rail and you will be fine."

Catriona stepped into the cold space and suppressed a quiver of cold as she pulled the door shut. She burrowed into the cloak's warmth thankful Salena had thought to include them in their excursion.

As she went deeper into the darkness, the dream burst in her mind—along with the eerie image of Duncan surrounded by black nothingness. Her heart thudded behind her ribs. She half expected flames to burst out and edge the black expanse. When it did not occur, she released a pent-up breath and shuddered, her voice reverberating against stone as she spoke.

"I do so pray ye are right."

Salena's tinkling laughter bounced off the rocky walls. "'Twill be fine. We are almost there."

Indeed, the damp, dark cold gave way to toasty warmth all aglow by the torchlit cave. Steam wafted upward glazing the rock-strewn, beamed ceiling with a dewy, glittery sheen. The scent of deep earth and minerals filled her lungs once again, just as they had that first day.

"Come, indulge with me," Salena said, shoving the cape off and drawing the gown over her head. She kicked off her boots and stood stark naked, the steam pluming up in spirals behind her. Turning, she sat upon the stony edge and dangled her slim legs in the water. Her expression turned wistful. "It always brings back memories to visit here. 'Twas a hot spring such as this one—though in the outdoors—where Falcon and I once made love in the beginning of our journey. John had even watched us—oh, it was such a wicked time!"

She thought of how they had watched she and John making love, and how Catriona had witnessed Falcon taking Salena in passion before her very eyes. Voyeurism, she concluded as her pussy began an incessant throb, proved to be an irresistibly sinful activity.

Catriona glanced across the large pool and located the opening to the corridor John had led her through the first time. They had not made love in these waters that eve, but had merely cleansed themselves from that first bout of phenomenal lovemaking. Now would be the time...not only with John, but with Falcon and Salena.

She swallowed a lump caught by the surge of her heartbeat. "All three of ye, ye are truly committed to one another, are ye not?" Catriona could not refrain. The incessant ache in her womb had her undressing hurriedly. She sat next to Salena, sighing when her chilled feet and lower legs were cradled by the steaming liquid. Her ass and labia pressed against the damp, rocky edge making her cunt go moist with excitement.

"Aye, very much so. But," she interjected, holding up a single finger, "I love Falcon and am bound to him by fate. John is a great friend and lover, a man I highly respect. As such, I am and always have been aware that one day, he will find his own mate of destiny. It is my feeling," she went on, lowering herself into the pool with a splash, "that we are all meant to come together at least once. In a sense, Falcon and I are releasing him to you once this foursome experiment has commenced and hopefully provides them both with supplemental powers."

Catriona slid into the pool, groaning when the bubbly hot liquid swallowed her into its heavenly haven. "Releasin' him to me?"

"Aye, releasing me to you."

The deep voice came from behind her. She spun in the water and looked up to find both John and Falcon standing fully nude on the ledge. It nearly brought her to her knees. The sight was one reminiscent of two Greek gods, one dark, one light, planted statuesque and powerful, as if they resided over a grand pool. The stone of their cocks jutted erect before them, their bodies corded and finely muscled in all the right places.

Catriona welcomed the rush of desire as it coursed through her blood. Centered in her pussy, the need tingled through her womb making her womanly juices flood out into the hot water.

"John..." Her gaze moved from one to the other. "Falcon."

Salena swam up behind her, she knew by the spatter of water, the scent of rose. "Are you feeling it, Catriona?" she whispered, and feminine arms circled her from behind.

"Aye, 'tis wanton, but inevitable at this point, I would say."

John and Falcon chuckled simultaneously. But seconds into the laughter, John's expression sobered. His moon-mist eyes glittered with animal need. "Cat...do you not know how much it pleases me to see you there, there in the water with Salena?"

As if to emphasize and encourage the point, Salena slid her hands up and around Catriona's shoulders and slowly pressed her breasts and abdomen against Catriona's back.

"And this, John? Does this not please you?" Salena purred.

To feel the soft, womanly curves glide over her skin, to hear the husky, feminine voice murmur in her ear, it left her utterly speechless when coupled with the sight before her. Here John stood, the breathtaking man she—somehow— already cared deeply for. He was positioned next to another gorgeous man, both in the nude. It made her swoon to think they would all be wrapped together in ecstasy very soon.

"You have no inkling just how much it does thrill me." John reached down and clasped his hand around his rod. Stroking himself, he said in a strangled voice, "And what of you, Catriona? Do you think you will be pleased by this naughty venture of ours?"

At first, the words would not dislodge from Catriona's throat. Salena's hand glided lower and cradled Catriona's breast. Her nipple went instantly hard against the tweaking and pinching Salena bestowed upon her. Her head fell back and she sighed, never taking her eyes from John's. The large swell of Salena's breast and taut nipples abraded across her back and shoulders. The carnal experience bombarded her ruthlessly, catapulting her into a sea of sin. But that was not even the beginning. When Salena found Catriona's pebble-hard clit, fluttering her fingertip over its bulk, she could not choke back the groan that escaped her lips. Fire burned through her blood as she watched both John and Falcon fondle their cocks at the very moment her own sex became a captive of this new game. There could be nothing more fascinatingly nefarious and yet, she soon found the vast possibilities bordered on endless.

"I-I cannot see how I could not be—oh!"

Salena sank a slim finger into Catriona's pussy. "Ah, gentlemen, our beautiful lady is drenched," she announced.

"Jesus!" Falcon dropped into the water feet-first. "Salena, for the love of the almighty, have pity upon my soul. You—you..." He shook his head as he pushed his way through the waist-high water. "You will be the death of me, after all, will you not, woman?"

Salena giggled, but it fast turned to a moan of anticipation as her husband neared. He snatched her from Catriona's back, settled her legs around his waist and buried his face in her ample breast.

As the two gasped and moaned just behind Catriona, John continued to rub his long cock. His steely gaze never left Catriona. She in turn stood dumbfounded, her stare locked on John as Salena once again draped herself behind Catriona. She welcomed the return of womanly softness, excited to have Salena at her back, and John's hard, sculpted body standing there for her eyes to feast upon. She rubbed her hand over Salena's arm as she spoke.

"John, I-I..."

"Catriona, love, 'tis your choice. But I beg of you," he said through clenched teeth, his body corded with restraint, "please make your decision posthaste, as I fear I cannot wait one moment longer to join you."

Just hearing the words, knowing he respected her enough to walk away, despite his obvious pained state, it made her heart flutter with both power and blessed submission. Duncan had never given her a choice. Lovemaking had always been at his insistence, on his schedule and in whatever manner he deemed *his* desire at the moment.

Recalling it so made her wonder how she had ever endured Duncan's touch. True, there had never been another man in her bed for comparison before. But now there most certainly had. And he stood before Catriona beseeching her to grant him permission to come to her. Ah, yet he wielded all the power in a mere look. Oh aye, merely by his quiet, commanding presence, by one blue-glazed, sensual look, he could spin her mind and body into a porridge-like mush.

Slowly, she lifted her hand from the water. "Come, me thief. Wait nae longer. I yearn for ye to join me—us—right here in this pool of steamin' lust."

John's eyes closed with relief. He groaned aloud just before diving into the water headlong. He made a brief splash and reemerged inches from her, his long, dark hair slicked back across his scalp. Droplets of moisture clung to his black lashes framing the stark mist of his eyes. Her gaze fell to his lips parted now as he breathed heavy through their sensual space. She longed to have that mouth graze over every inch of her body, explore every curve and crevice. Just imagining it made her shiver and sent a renewed flood of heat to her loins.

"You have just made me the happiest man in all of this world." John planted his feet on the bottom of the pool and reached for Catriona. His hands cradled her face and he drew her into a kiss of wet, decadent seduction. She dueled with his tongue while welcoming the sweet sword of it into her mouth. Ah, but she felt she would die of thirst if she did not get more of him—nay, *all* of him—into her very soul!

Falcon grunted, pressing his body against Salena's back. "Make that two of the happiest men."

"Turn around, Catriona," Salena murmured. "We shall attempt to increase the powers they receive by sealing one another in a kiss as our men ravish us from behind. Hopefully, the connection will give them more sustenance than ever before."

John did not seem quite ready to release her. "Mmm, I fear I will lose myself before I even get inside you," he said to

Catriona as he gripped her hips. He lifted her just enough to abrade her pussy over his hard cock. It made her eyes snap wide. She heard her own intake of breath followed by a quickening deep in her belly. Catriona's vagina moistened, releasing more warm fluid into the water.

She wound her arms around his neck surer now than ever before. And, oh, how she longed to give him that extraordinary power Salena spoke of, to play a part in gifting him with a depth of energy he had yet to ever experience.

"I surrender, John, to ye, to them, to us all. I want more than anythin' to feed yer sorcerer's soul." She nipped his lower lip between her teeth and reveled in the groan she easily wrought from him. "And I desire once again to experience yer prowess and to feel ye inside me."

"Cat..." he breathed, kissing her nose, her cheeks, her forehead. The tender gesture further sealed her emotions and made her skin tingle with need. "I am honored by your pledge. You have given me such pleasure already. I am such a blessed man."

"John," Salena whispered. "Turn her to face me...please."

Before John could do as Salena bade, Catriona spun in the water, eager for this fascinating joining. She saw that Falcon now stood at Salena's back and devoured her neck. One of his large hands skimmed and kneaded her full breasts, the other dove deep to search for her pussy. Salena's eyes were half open in bliss, her arms draped up and behind her so she could cling to Falcon's neck. Her long sable mane spun in the bubbly water around her in a starkly contrasted mixture with Falcon's golden tresses. The two of them made a breathtaking, beautiful picture. Just watching another man and woman in the intimate embrace while in such close proximity made Catriona's blood race through her veins.

Salena released her hold on Falcon and held her arms out in welcome. "Come, Catriona. I am eager to see what 'tis like to taste a woman, to feel slick, bare breasts pressed to mine."

John and Falcon swore in tortured unison.

"I must admit to a curiosity, meself." Catriona floated into Salena's arms, the hot water lapping around them. Nipple to nipple, the curve of their breasts came together. Salena's rosy scent floated up to tempt Catriona as she wrapped her arms around Salena's small but curvy frame and pulled her closer. "Mmm, 'tis nice. Ye feel so verra soft against me skin."

"Mmm-hmm, very pleasant," Salena said on a pant. "Oh God, I am getting wet already." She ducked her head and burned a hot path of kisses from Catriona's shoulder, up the slope of her neck to the corner of her mouth.

"Christ Jesus, you ladies will drive me mad before I can even absorb your energies." John gripped Catriona's hips and drew her lower body toward him as she leaned forward toward Salena. Falcon did the same so that the two women lay almost stomach-down, making a connected bridge between the men.

"Ah, you both look delectable!" Falcon exclaimed, his eyes rolling back in his head.

Salena wrapped her arms around Catriona's shoulders, while Catriona explored Salena's smooth, supple back. She looked deep into the azure, aroused orbs of another woman. Another subtle puff of Salena's floral scent rose up to fill Catriona's nostrils. Her mouth watered and she longed for her first taste of woman. From behind her, she could feel the hard grip of John's hands. He guided her legs and wrapped them around his hips, dragging the head of his cock down her slit as he did so.

"Oh…oh, this does feel nice," she whispered, gasping for air.

Salena nodded, allowing Falcon to mold her lower body to his in much the same manner. "Mmm, aye, now kiss me. I want to feel your lips on mine while Falcon enters me with his big rod."

Catriona experienced her first passionate, female kiss. Her senses snapped off in a blast of fire as if a kettle of lard boiled around her. Supple, sweet lips moved tender and hungry over hers, while John's cock probed her cunt. The small tongue fluttered with potent talent, spinning Catriona into a whole different level of desire.

Upper body now held buoyant upon the water, she ran her hands up and down Salena's back. Salena did the same, but her caressing trek moved around until she filled both palms with Catriona's breasts. It sent Catriona careening into a whole new flight of lust when Salena pinched her nipples at the exact moment John entered her.

Catriona tore her mouth from Salena's. "Holy—oh my God!" John's finger found her throbbing bud. She was already so close to climax, her head spun with giddiness.

Salena dragged Catriona's mouth back to hers. "Ah, I want more kisses—*oh!*" She jolted against Catriona's lips when Falcon tore into her from behind. Their mouths clashed. Both men sang out a moan of animal ecstasy. A perfect rhythm evolved as John entered Catriona in harmony with Falcon's retreat from Salena. They swung as one, forward and back, forward and back. Despite the movement, Catriona's lips remained sealed with Salena's as they devoured each other's mouths, their arms clinging to one another.

Catriona had never felt such an all-encompassing bliss before this wondrous coupling. She could not drink in enough of Salena's flavor, could not get John deep enough into her core. She clenched her legs around his hips slamming him into her core while drinking of Salena's flavor. Curiosity and maddening desire drove her to explore Salena's full breasts. Ah, what wondrous sensations, to lift the weight of a breast in your hand, to feel the taut nipple scraping over your palm and hear the gentle moans of a woman's song in your ear!

Water sloshed around the four bodies. Salena screamed into Catriona's mouth and clutched her tighter so that she was forced to release Salena's silky mounds. Their heads rose higher and their breasts touched again. Nipples flicked against nipples. The desperation rose and Catriona grappled for Falcon so that she could press Salena closer. She groaned her need as her tongue continued to pummel Salena's sweet, warm mouth.

"Aye, I hear you, milady, and I wholeheartedly agree." Falcon raced his palms up Salena's sides and reached out, drawing and holding Catriona against his wife. Ah, the maddening relief of it! If it were possible to warm her flesh any further, it did so now. The move forced Salena to release her legs from around Falcon. Buoyant with Falcon's huge cock still inside her, Salena clambered up and clamped her legs around Catriona's hips. It jolted Catriona's legs from around John, but John recovered quickly and cleverly by sliding up closer to her ass. It allowed Salena room to pull John nearer with her legs and arms, while her lips remained sealed to Catriona's and her breasts melded to Catriona's tingling ones.

Pressed now between John and Salena—with Falcon's hard shoulders beneath her palms—she felt much like a slab of meat between twin slices of bread. John's cock was so very long it stayed buried inside her, despite the more upright position she found herself in. Her pussy muscles clamped down on him, squeezing, stroking.

Catriona clenched Falcon's shoulders tighter, her mouth still sealed to Salena's, and pushed backward toward John. Pleasure such as she had never encountered before, teased her every sense. His enormous penis touched her in places so deep, so sensitive, she thought she would soar to the moon at any moment. She tasted the flavor of a woman's hungering kiss, smelled the scent of pure water laced with heated sex juice and perspiration. Catriona marveled at the contrast between soft feminine flesh and all-male muscle, and did her best to explore at every opportunity. She opened her eyes, and through the rising steam, she caught flashes of Salena's beautiful face, and Falcon's contorted, ecstasy-washed expression over Salena's shoulder.

It was all so very carnal and hedonistic. The taboo of what she participated in served to further feed her ardor. Her pulse thudded painfully in her throat making it difficult to draw air into her lungs. Catriona honed in on the heat and hardness of John behind her, the way he worshipped her body, caressed her with such loving care and expertise. The knowledge that she shared it all with John left her breathless, he a man who had become so very close to her heart in such a short time, as if they had known one another since the beginning of time. Emotions of euphoria and awe overwhelmed her, and she longed for this experience to go on and on, to never, ever end.

Wildly curious, she skimmed her palm down Salena's side and forced her hand down between their bellies to the spot where Salena had perched her pussy. Ah, yes, miraculously, Falcon's long manhood was still rooted in Salena's passage, despite the angle she was now held by being pressed almost flush to Catriona's front side. Catriona fluttered her fingers over Salena's clit, down to the portion of Falcon's cock that barely remained outside her. She caressed them both in a circular motion, first silky folds, then down to the granite hardness of another man's sex and balls. They both groaned their satisfaction, increasing the tempo of the dance. The naughtiness of what she did made Catriona's entire body threaten to buckle and drown.

John whispered Catriona's name over and over, his left arm sliding between the female stomachs as he pulled Catriona to him, his right hand exploring all four breasts in succession. Arms tightened, cocks rammed harder, deeper. Pussies and mouths thirsted, reaching for more, for all.

"Mmm..." Now beyond coyness, propriety long forgotten, Catriona devoured Salena's mouth, welcoming the first vague waves of climax. She glanced right, then left, saw that John and Falcon reached for one another. Their large hands clasped one another's forearms making an enclosed circle around her and Salena. Her own arms slid around Salena to hold her close and continue the kiss.

Glancing up and around, she saw that Falcon threw his head back and reared his pelvis forward so that he could pummel his wife with profound penetration. She knew John mimicked the same act by the sudden jolt that nearly had her teeth gnashing into Salena's. Her pussy spasmed in a teasing prelude of what would soon come. A collective male groan echoed against the cave walls. Firelight from the torches danced upon varying shades of flesh. Steam seemed to increase its density, swirling up almost magically around the foursome.

That was when Catriona felt it, like a never-ending zap of lightning. Ecstasy such as she had never before experienced catapulted from John's cock, through her cunt and up into her tongue. Salena screamed into Catriona's mouth and increased the kiss with a frantic clutch of her shoulders. Her fingers tangled in Catriona's hair forcing her to deepen the kiss. It seemed Salena tore the very air from Catriona's lungs. Catriona fought back, now in a frenzy for more. A spark of energy raced back and forth. It traveled from Falcon's cock, through Salena and Catriona's sealed mouths. It continued down the length of her body to John's penis where he relentlessly pounded into Catriona's pussy.

"Oh, yes! Holy son of a..." John growled it out, his taut body quivering behind Catriona's. She could hear his ragged breathing as he spilled shot after shot of semen into her vagina. Still clasping arms, John and Falcon's knuckles whitened. Catriona watched in awe as the light passed between them, again and again.

"Lorcan alive, I cannot take the ecstasy much longer!" Falcon's voice boomed in the lovers' lair. His breath came out in a mixed cry of pain and pleasure.

Caught in her own endless web of euphoria, Catriona was loath to break the kiss, for she now knew these wizard lovers required this connection in order to extract their immortal powers. She thought she would go mad with the endless orgasms, her own whimpers muffled into a duet with Salena's.

The hot, pumping lust burned through every cell of her body wrenching sighs and gasps from deep in her lungs.

Just when she thought she could take the rapture no longer, the cycles tapered away. John and Falcon let out a final sigh and released each other's limbs. Catriona slowly withdrew her mouth from Salena's. Eyes fluttered in disbelief. Breathing slowed into long, deep inhalations. John withdrew and guided her down so her feet touched the stone bottom. Falcon did the same to Salena. Almost as if instinct drove her, Catriona spun so that she faced John. She listened to the swish of water as Salena also turned to her man.

"John..." Catriona held his cheek, the stubble tickling the palm of her hand. "I do not ken exactly what has just happened, but I am honored to have been a part of it."

He gathered her close, his still-hard cock pressed alongside her abdomen. His eyes glowed like twin cerulean flames in the firelit space. She noted how his skin seemed to shine with a new glow of energy, as if his soul had been ignited and overflowed from his core. Lowering his head, he kissed her with tenderness, his mouth warm, wet and tasting of ale. It made her heart still to see that look of impassioned emotion in his eyes.

"Thank you," he whispered, his voice choked. "Your gift, along with Salena's collaboration, has given me and my soul-brother the most phenomenal store of immortal energy ever in our existence. I do not know why we never once thought to include a fourth person for added power. Perhaps," he rasped, his fingers combing through her damp locks, "it was because we waited for you."

The implications of his words made her knees go weak. She wound her arms around his thick neck and leapt up in the water so that she could straddle him. God, she could not get close enough to this man! What an addictive temptation he had proven to be.

"Waited for me, ye say?" She kissed his neck tasting the saltiness of flesh there where his pulse continued to beat erratically. "Such a patient mon to wait for all those centuries for one bonny, Scottish lass such as meself. One, nae less, reputed to be a witch in pursuit by a king's determined army."

"Witch, aye," he grinned, kneading her ass cheeks and making the sparse hair on her arms stand on end. "I suspect those very 'witch' abilities—those you possess to speak to the dead—added the perfect ingredient Falcon and I required yet were unaware of needing all this time."

"I was glad to be of service, kind sir," she mocked, grinding her pussy across the front of his waning erection.

"Was?" Falcon chimed in. "By Jove, if I have anything a'tall to say about the matter, 'twill not be merely in the past but an ongoing, forever event."

Salena wrapped herself around Falcon as she fed on his wide shoulders and taut nipples. "More, I need more."

Falcon hissed, "Woman, you are incorrigible!"

Salena giggled, not letting up on her pursuit, but Falcon's words of forever did not become lost in the play. Catriona's abdomen twisted into tight knots of regret when his meaning sank in. Aye, this had been an amazing interlude, one she wished she could repeat until her dying days. But the fact of the matter was, Catriona Graham, a Gypsy condemned as a witch by the king of Scotland, could stay no longer. To remain here would put all of John's loyal staff, and any of Falcon's Merry Men in the vicinity, in unnecessary danger. Falcon and John, she knew, would be able to fend for themselves, for their immortality and sorcerers' powers alone protected them. But there were definitely others to consider...such as Salena.

It was Catriona's understanding that the wearing of the *Centaurus* pendant was the only thing—besides Falcon's love and protection—that kept Salena safe from harm or death. And what if the magical amulet were stolen from Salena or destroyed by the king's vindictive soldiers while in search of Catriona? Nay, Catriona refused to be responsible for Salena's life and that of so many others. She would not put anyone in harm's way for her own selfish desires. Oh, but the thought of departing from this heaven, of leaving behind this extraordinary man whom she feared she was falling in love with…it made her violently ill to look ahead to that grim future.

"What is wrong, my love?" John whispered, tipping up her chin so that she was forced to look through the swirling hot vapor into his penetrating stare.

"Ye ken 'tis best…ye see, I cannot—"

"Falcon! John!" The deep male voice echoed through the far rocky corridor. A tall graying man of about three score in years emerged. He wore the garb of a forest brigand, a feathered woodsman's hat upon his head. But it was not the longbow slung across his wide back nor the sword belted to the waist of his braies that gave him away. It was the tone of respect and alarm for Falcon and John that revealed him to be one of Falcon's cohorts.

John's gaze swung to the man. He removed Catriona's naked body from his person and set her behind him in the water, blocking her from the man's view. "Lance, what troubles you, man?"

"Riders." He planted a hand on the wall of the cave, bending to catch his breath. "It appears several wear the royal doublet of the Scots king. The others, they are each garbed in tartans of varying allegiances."

"How many in their party?"

"A score and ten at least, milord. A thoroughly armed, well mounted and somewhat uniformed troupe," he added, swallowing audibly.

Catriona's pulse lurched. "Nae, please, nae…" She backed away, splashing toward the opposite side of the pool.

"Catriona," John barked. "Return to my side at once."

"Nae," she repeated in a whisper, shaking her head. "They have found me. I-I must be gone from here before they do ye all harm for harborin' a convicted witch. I must—"

"Witch?" Lance blurted out.

"You are safe here," Salena offered, ignoring Lance's surprise as she swam toward Catriona.

"Get back!" Catriona held up a hand and made her way to the far ledge. She climbed from the water and, heedless of her naked state, briskly dried herself off with a towel from a nearby stack of linens. Sidling to where her clothing and boots lay, she gathered up the items and clutched them to her bare skin. "All of ye must not prevent me from fleein'."

"Lance, secure the drawbridge at once." John started for the underwater stairs, his eyes never leaving Catriona as he pushed through the pool.

"Aye, 'tis already done. But, masters, you are aware we are few within the keep? Most of our band rides out on skirmishes for the coming night's raids. And some, as you know, remain behind at Falcon's Wyngate Hall."

John stopped briefly, angling in the water to acknowledge the man's point. "Understood, Lance. Go now and man the gatehouse, and do not let anyone in or out. May your god go with you, loyal friend."

"Consider it done, sir." Lance turned on his booted heels and disappeared up the passageway.

"Falcon," John said as he crossed to the edge of the pool where his garments remained in a heap upon the ledge. "We must see everyone to safety. The servants, our ladies..."

"Aye, my brother, I am right here with you. Let us be on our way." Falcon drew himself up out of the water followed by Salena. They stood naked and proud before one another as they dried off with linen towels supplied at intervals throughout the springhouse. He nipped Salena in the chin and kissed her in a swift yet thorough manner. "You know where to go, love. See that Catriona and all the staff are removed to the hidden chambers."

Salena drew on her gown and nodded. "As always and forever, you can count on me, husband."

"Catriona!" John shouted across the cave as he leapt from the spring and jammed on his braies. "Return to my side at once. My God, lady, do not drive an immortal to his grave. 'Tis imperative that you come here now and follow Salena to safety. Please, do as you are bid!"

It seemed as if a sharpened lance tore through her heart. Oh, how she longed to run to him, to stay in his arms until her dying day, to hole up for eternity with him in that safe lair Falcon spoke of. But it just was not to be. She could not change the fact that she was a criminal, a woman wanted for witchcraft offenses against the Scottish crown. No one, not even these immortal, seemingly invincible warlocks could change that.

Nay, no amount of magic could save her, and the truth remained that other peoples' lives depended on what decision she made at this very instant. Aye, she had been gifted with some sort of sixth sense since birth, one that allowed her to speak to the dead. But never did she wish in the future to be speaking to those who had passed on due to her current selfish choices.

So when John hardened his expression and pierced her with his narrowed gaze, she swung around and charged naked into the black passageway at the far end of the cave. She heard his footsteps as he started after her, but it was too late. Catriona quickly became lost in the dark bowels of Sedgewick Castle.

# Chapter Six

## ဆ

She clung to her garments with one hand and felt her way along the rock wall with the other. Water dribbled down her back making her nipples go hard and goose bumps prickle over her entire body. Catriona ignored all the discomforts, well used to harsh travels afoot. Instead, she narrowed her eyes and strained to see in the dim passageway. The channel seemed to twist and turn and shoot off in many different directions, but she pushed on, determined to put a safe distance between herself and John.

Catriona plodded forward, her heart aching, threatening to burst from her chest. Love—or something very close to it— warmed her soul when the handsome vision of him swam before her. Tears stung her eyes for she sensed it was highly likely she might never know his touch again, might never lay eyes on that perfect specimen of a man.

"Enough," she whispered, and focused on putting as much distance as possible between her and the man she longed to run to more than anyone or anything else in her entire life.

When she was sure she had lost him, she stopped and first drew on her braies and boots. Her feet were numb and damp, and she sighed inwardly when the wool lining cradled her feet. Shivering, she slid into the shirt and jerkin, and swirled the cloak around her trembling body, grateful Salena had suggested she bring the wrap when she had enticed her to the underground spring.

Catriona moved deeper into nothingness, fumbling her way along the cool, clammy walls. She inhaled, suddenly sensing the aroma of fresh air over that of the musky scent that hung in the tunnels. Intuitively, she closed her eyes and inhaled, following the trail. The channel grew narrower, and at first, Catriona feared she had erred in her intuition. But then she felt the burst of cold air and pulled up the cape's hood, trembling when the chilly gust swirled around her wet head. Her teeth chattered but she trudged onward, shoving aside the memory of a warm bed and even warmer hospitality from them all, of an emotion between her and John she could only call love. Again, she coaxed herself to focus on the mission at hand. A few more steps took her around a sharp bend where she could see a round opening of daylight far ahead. She sighed in relief, yet one last time, her heart ached and her feet longed to turn and retrace her steps back into the arms of her handsome thief and his fascinating triangle with Salena and Falcon.

"Nae, Catriona," she whispered to herself as she drew the wrap snug against the chill and trotted toward the light. "'Tis best for all concerned if ye flee this place and leave not a trace of yerself behind."

The opening widened as she neared. Winter's bite whooshed up her cloak and nipped at her still-damp skin. She groaned, recalling the soothing, penetrating heat of the luxurious spring bath not an hour ago. Though the sky shone pristine blue, the sun angling sharp from the west, a dark cloud hung ominous on the northern horizon. Yet here, the sun persevered and made a glaze of diamond-like crystals glitter across the surface of the freshly fallen snow. Despite the bright cast to the sky, the winter winds moaned stormy around her. Catriona secured the cape's hood to protect her damp head and ran out into the deep snow.

She glanced over her shoulder as she fled, her feet and legs sinking into the cold depths, and saw that the outer fortress walls loomed above her. Somehow, the underground passageway had wound its way down and under the stone wall and moat of the keep. She wondered briefly if John knew his otherwise impenetrable fortress appeared to be compromised in brief favor of his foes due to this tunnel's access. But there was not time to ponder it any longer. Catriona veered off into the concealing safety of the forest.

No sooner had she approached the edge of the woods than the hoofbeats thundered up behind her. She whirled toward the sound, taken aback by the sudden noise. Shading her eyes from the bright sunlight, she looked up at the ominous outline of a man upon a great steed. Blinded by the sun, the man's face and silhouette blurred to her vision. But a sense of doom and vague familiarity ate at her gut when he pulled back on the reins forcing his mount to prance in place.

"Who...who goes there?" Her voice came out in a squeak of fear. The moment of cowardice mortified her yet she could not rid herself of the dry knot in her throat, or soften the pounding of her heart. She could hear shouts in the distance, other riders. But it was just this one who had found her, who almost dared her to run in order to begin a cat-and-mouse chase.

Seconds passed. The volatile winds stirred her cloak and further chilled her damp tresses. Her body began to shudder uncontrollably. She caught the scent of horse and distant wood smoke mixed with danger. Then he spoke.

"Hello, wife."

Her heart leapt from her chest. Catriona gulped, the forest spinning around her. She stumbled back and leaned against a tree trunk just when he moved into the shade. Indeed, Duncan McNicol of the clan Nicol sat mounted before her on a stallion so fine, it could be from none other than the king's stables. He leaned upon the high pommel of his saddle, his wrists crossed leisurely.

"D-Duncan?" she croaked.

He straightened and threw his head back, a deep rumble escaping his clamped teeth. "Surprised, dear Catriona?"

"B-but...nae." She pressed her spine into the bark of the tree to ground herself from the dizziness that whirled in her head. With a hunger for continued consciousness, she dragged blessed air into her scorching lungs. "I-I saw ye burn at the stake nearly a year past. I saw it with me verra own eyes."

Her pulse thundered with fear and renewed confusion when he urged the horse forward. He leaned down, his red and gold plaid flaring across his knee, and traced her cheek with his gloved finger. The gesture somehow made her stomach churn, made her long to take flight, if only he did not impede her retreat...

"Me dear Catriona. Ye always were such a clueless, drivelin' lass."

She gasped at the insult and tore her face from his touch. "How dare ye?"

"How dare I?" He canted his head mocking her in a haughty demeanor she had never seen him exhibit before. "I merely speak the truth, ye whore."

She sucked in another shocked breath but he ignored her and went on. "Aye, I saw ye that day spreadin' yer legs for the sorcerer, nearly ruttin' upon the bloodied snow. 'Tis me good fortune that one of me men kent of this mon who announced himself to be John Lawton, kent him to be from the thievin' band of brigands terrorizin' England. We journeyed here straightaway after locatin' a fellow near the border who kent him to be residin' here. It seems this wizard lover of yers is now due for an execution, as well...since I witnessed his witchcraft me verra self."

"Nae..."

"Oh, aye, healin' of fatal wounds and disappearances into thin air. Mmm, 'tis more than enough to throw him before James and see that the chap is convicted and burned to death."

She shook her head violently, images of John burning at the stake flashing before her eyes. Her stomach ached and churned with dread even though she had been assured of John's immortal state of being. "He is an Englishmon! The Scots king has nae jurisdiction, nae right."

When he merely smirked, she added weakly, "Please, nae."

He snorted, continuing to inform her of his cruel plans. "Ye see, capturin' another witch — the king does not give a fuck about nationality — will further ingratiate me to the king. Nae doubt 'twill have him rewardin' me with quite a profitable bonus, in addition to that I had prior been promised for implicatin' and bringin' *ye* and yer Gypsies in, love."

She managed mere disdain in lieu of the profanities she longed to hurl at him. "Do not *ever* call me yer love again! And the truth, ye say? I have yet to hear it from ye, *husband* — nae, liar. Pray tell, do so enlighten me. How is it that ye accomplished yer own death, yet here ye sit astride before me as one of the king's puppet soldiers? Mayhap by the verra witchcraft ye claimed to be possessin' for yerself durin' our unfortunate marriage, Duncan — or perhaps by a blackguard, coward's deceit?"

The sting across her cheek lessened only by the sharp pain that burst in her head. It snapped back, crashing into the tree as stars swam across her vision. She held her cheek and glared up at him. "Ye evil, *vile* bastard!"

The wicked gleam that glowed in his eyes when he bellowed made her long to vomit. "Aye, come to think on it, better an evil bastard than a promiscuous harlot, would not ye be sayin', love?"

She tried to step away from the tree but he sidled the steed up closer, blocking her escape. "What do ye want, Duncan? Do be gettin' on with yer maliciousness before I scream and alert the entire keep."

"Why, I want ye, dear wife. And might I add that yer screams will bring about me own troops for ye to contend with, as well as the possible death of yer lover's servants?"

Her heart sank, for he seemed to have all the answers she did not wish to hear. "Why, Duncan? Why do ye do this terrible thing to me? Ye once claimed to love me. Ye masqueraded as me lovin' husband—" she quivered in revulsion, "and much as it repulses me now, ye took me to yer bed each night."

Sudden lust glittered in his eyes further enhancing her nausea. "Aye, and a delectable piece of meat ye could be at times. But 'tis simple, me dear. I hunt ye down at the king's request, of course. Ye are sentenced to die by burnin' upon return to North Berwick. Yer crimes against the crown cannot go unpunished. And though I have yet to witness them meself, I've decided to testify I've seen them just to be done with ye…and earn a few extra gold coins, of course."

"I did not play a part in the attempted sinkin' of King James and his wife Anne's ship, and ye well ken it! 'Twas a sheer coincidence. And even if it were not so, I still did not participate in the group of witches whom coalesced and wished ill upon the king and his bride. They were not even a part of me people."

"Catriona, I have seen many a thing—odd occurrences with yer Gypsy people—since before we married. 'Twas why I married ye, to be the king's eyes and ears and further assist in eradicatin' those who threatened to harm our most royal ruler. I undertook a most noble mission, ye see? The king ordered our union for that verra cause, so that I could witness yer powers—*their* powers—and bring ye all to justice. Yer supposed ability to communicate with the dead, and their evil spells and hexes whispered about across all of Scotland, are priority issue with James. Ye are all witches who deserve to die for yer tyranny against the crown. So there ye have it, witch Graham." He shrugged. "'Tis plain and simple."

"Ye stayed with me for months without witnessin' me…abilities. Ye even claimed to have powers of yer own."

"Do not be an idiot! 'Twas all a front to ensure me place in yer lowly Gypsy band for as long as 'twould take to witness yer evil and see all ye misfits dead."

Shock and anger made her long to reach up and slap the smirk from his mouth, but instead, she dug her nails into her palms. The wind tossed his severely cut auburn hair around his harsh features, and she wondered how she had ever thought him handsome. She had experienced his hurried, almost clumsy touch time and again, and had thought it love, had even talked herself into enjoying it at times just to please him, thinking this was the normal way of man and wife. And all the while, he had been playing her for a fool? He was nothing but a spy sent by the king to seek out and entrap all those suspected of witchcraft in opposition to His Royal Highness?

She spoke through her teeth. "Tell me, how and when did ye come to be in the king's employ?"

"A verra long time ago, well before we met." He grinned, but the smile did not reach his beady eyes.

His response did not surprise her, and she no longer cared. Even before this shocking revelation and his return from the dead, she had begun to let go of him…or the love for him she now knew to be false. Thoughts of John gave her strength, and she realized at that moment of great comparison that she truly did love John Lawton.

*Nae, there could not be a comparison between this reprehensible ogre and the lovin', carin' mon who saved me life twice now in but a week's time.*

"I'll be thinkin' I've gone daft if ye do not enlighten me, *beloved* husband. If ye please, answer one last question…"

He sighed theatrically and glanced toward the sky, his tone condescending. "All right, I shall indulge ye just this once before we get this return journey to North Berwick underway."

"What went amiss? Who was it that I watched die at the stake there next to me verra own ma—me ma *ye* had murdered?"

He grinned, his eyes as cold as the snow around them. "'Twas me twin brother, Geoffry."

Bile rose in her throat. Catriona had not known he had a twin brother, or that she had married such a cruel monster until this day. The reality of her marriage being a farce boiled deep in her soul, along with the anger and hatred that simmered there. God help her, she had gone willingly abed with a man who would see his own brother and her mother burned without batting an eye? Was that why his family had suddenly disowned her, because they blamed her for their son's death?

Catriona reached around the tree for leverage as her head spun with maddening speed. Beneath the concealment of her cape, she stepped a foot to the side in preparation to bolt as soon as the horse shifted its weight away from her.

"Ye murdered yer own flesh and blood? And ye kent yer 'wife' and all of the townspeople thought it to be ye, and grieved yer passin'?"

"Aye. I could not go on pretendin' to be a sorcerer in yer Gypsy band any longer. Yer ma and I, we argued. She found me out, and in so doin', implicated herself in the attempt to down the king's ship by witchcraft and—"

"Nae, 'tis a lie! She would not—she did not admit to any such thing!"

He shrugged. "Matters not now one way or the other. But I could not stand to live with ye and yer filthy people any longer. So I thought to 'murder' meself in hopes of bringin' forth more acts of ye and yer Gypsy peoples' rebellion and sinful witchcraft out of the woodwork. But instead, ye all withdrew into yerselves as if ye kent somethin' was amiss. Eventually, after me 'death', I received word from me local spies that they had actually witnessed many more acts of defiant witchcraft against The Crown, and had seen ye, as well, performin' séances...to reach yer ma and meself." He added a sarcastic chuckle to that.

"Did they, now?" She forced as much of her own sarcasm into her tone as she could muster.

He winked, his dark eyes resembling two chips of coal in the pale plane of his face. "That they did, lass. So me brother's sacrifice proved to be a profitable, justified one, ye see?"

She clenched the cloak's opening shut, warding off the chill with one hand. But with the other, she planned for freedom, reaching around the ancient oak in preparation to bolt. "Ah, I see me embarrassment—or rather, me instincts, now that I reflect on it—were founded. Had I performed a séance in yer presence, ye would have hauled me—yer verra own wife—off to prison, would ye not have, Duncan?"

"Aye. Either that or I would have tired of me role and set ye up in some manner in which yer guilt would have been apparent for all to document. Now enough. 'Tis time for us to be on our way."

"Nae, I refuse to go with ye peaceably. As ye can see, I stand upon English soil. Hence, I seek protection and asylum by the crown of the English queen." She ground her teeth together and shot him her most loathing stare. "Now get the devil out of me way, ye heartless bastard."

Duncan's jaw snapped shut and his sharp-featured face went ashen with ire. She enjoyed the briefest moment of verbal revenge. But brief it proved to be. Catriona sensed his intent to yank her up onto his horse, so she kneed the underbelly of the steed to foil his attempt. The horse neighed and reared up in protest, hooves pummeling the air. The sudden flurry took Duncan by surprise and nearly unseated him. It was the opportunity Catriona had been waiting for. She faltered but for a split second, then tore out across the forest, her pulse booming in her head, her booted feet pounding through the deep snow.

Just when she gloried in sweet escape, pain ripped through her scalp. He had her by the hair and jerked her up onto the stallion. Forced to lie stomach-down across his lap, the jolt of the horse's gait drove her breath from her lungs. The ground flew by in a fog beneath the steed's wild, galloping hooves. And Catriona knew a terror to rival that of a witch's burning stake.

* * * * *

Lorcan watched from his place behind a towering, snow-dappled elm. "*Nay!*"

It tore from his chest and echoed out across the frozen lake, out and away from the walls of John's keep. He had not counted on the Gypsy woman being quite so stubborn and protective of John at the same time, enough so to flee in order to ensure John's safety. Pacing back and forth, Lorcan wore a path in the snow clean through to the frozen, dead foliage beneath, his robe and beard fluttering in the bitter-cold winds. Snow clouds churned in the distant sky slowly painting a dull gray over the pristine beauty of a clear winter's day. And like those storm clouds, his immortal heart roiled with sickening, helpless worry and a sense of forever doom.

One lone tear trickled over his leathery cheek. Oh, how he despised this skin, this gnarled, heinous body! When would this madness—this *hell*—ever end? The thirteenth century seemed an eternity ago. Heartache. It would forever be impressed in his essence as the era of heartache. The spell cast upon him for his horrible transgressions now approached nearly *four hundred* years! God help him, if he could go back in time and undo what malice and mayhem he had caused, he would do it in a second's time. To be cursed in retaliation with eternal life in a body far from one's own, oh, but it was the epitome of hell at its absolute worst! Being forced with haphazard wizard's powers and foresight into the future— foresight that turned out half the time to be misread by the jumbled old mind he had been encumbered with. It was enough to make him give in to the witch who had sought revenge and forced him into this eternal misery.

A howl tore from his gut as a future vision of Catriona Graham burning at the stake suddenly flashed in his mind.

"Nay... It cannot be." He tossed aside his staff and fell to his knees screaming, "*Damn* you, Desmona!" He clenched his fists and shook them at the oncoming clouds. "I give in. Take my black soul. Tear my heart from this ugly chest you burdened me with. I don't give a bloody hell anymore."

A husky, noxious laughter reverberated around Lorcan, but as usual, he could only hear her, could only sense the venom all around him. The craven witch, he grumbled silently. She had not shown her evil face to him since that fateful day in 1238 A.D. during her odious alliance with King Henry III and the casting of this endless spell upon Lorcan. The king had taken away the rights of those English barons — Lorcan's father being one of many — who had sought more voice in the king's state affairs. A bloody feud ensued in which the witch Desmona remained aligned with King Henry, creating mayhem against the barons and their families. Consequently, there had been a huge rift between Desmona and Lorcan that had only fueled the flames of the war.

*"Ah, so you wish to die, to never be given another chance at a normal life?"*

He spoke through the sobs, feeling the tears freeze into crystal droplets on his face. "Aye. Strike me dead this instant! No more. I cannot take this torture anymore."

She made a tsking sound. *"Such heart-wrenching, almost repenting sadness from one as back-stabbing as yourself."*

"Now, Goddamn it! *Now!*" Lorcan lowered his fists to the snow and pressed his face in its relentless cold. He wanted that. He wanted to go numb, to no longer have to search for a spell-breaker, to never have to recall the anguish of lost love again. *"Well, if you insist. But have you forgotten... If you request for the spell to be broken suicidally, then you take the lives of your protégés with you. Not to mention breaking the hearts of those they both love, and the many countless followers and unfortunate people who love and respect them."*

Lorcan groaned. He rubbed his face deeper into the icy snow. His tired old mind drifted back to the day the spell had begun. It was the day Desmona had spewed her wrath. She had randomly chosen Falcon and John as Lorcan's charges to be burdened with. At the time, both had been newborn babes Lorcan had not even known at the time. Immortality had been cast upon Falcon and John both at the same time Desmona had put it upon Lorcan so that his responsibilities and commitments would be never-ending. As a person of royal descent suddenly transformed into a drifter and put into the party of Falcon and John's nomadic families, Lorcan had grudgingly become their vassal seeing them through the death of family, friends, lovers and enemies alike over the years.

The fateful first day, Desmona briefed Lorcan on his newly acquired, sporadic powers, and gleefully informed him he would be trapped in this old body into endless eternity. Out of some sick sense of delight, she had randomly selected sorcerer powers for John and Falcon, predetermining their unique forces. Each magical ability had emerged and matured as each child had grown into adulthood. Their soul-brother status and need for triad sex in order to keep them together throughout time had eventually come with manhood.

As the years passed back in that era, Lorcan had watched both John and Falcon grow from adorable bouncing babies into strikingly handsome, strong and righteous men in charge of their own party of avengers. After being murdered by King Henry's son, Edward, in 1265, Simon De Montfort, leader of the barons in opposition to the king, left behind many loyal followers. Their new twenty-seven-year-old leader, Falcon Montague—eventually known as Robin Hood—and his loyal partner John Lawton, had led the deceased De Montfort's followers into the forest and formed their legendary outlaw band. Lorcan had remained with his charges, following nomadically along, working on his magic to find that solution to counteract the spell.

But Lorcan had been unable to give in to Desmona's hatred and accept his fate. He had worked and worked on his craft until he had finally come up with a possible spell of his own, an antidote to Desmona's curse. It was a remedy that would undo Desmona's evil spell, but only after both of his charges—and then Lorcan himself—had found their eternal mates. He had conjured up first the *Centaurus* medallion. And by God, it had worked, bringing Salena into Falcon's life and gifting her with immortality. He now struggled to guide John onto the correct path to achieve the *Scorpian* and search for its corresponding partner whom he had hoped until now was the Scottish lass Catriona Graham. Regardless of the *Scropian's* outcome, Falcon and John had both turned out to be "sons" Lorcan could be proud of. He supposed, after running it all through his weary mind again, he had done *something* right over the centuries.

But doing one thing correct for once did not give him the right to end their lives, did it? Falcon now had his beloved Salena. John had been struck with the uniqueness of Catriona, though it was looking as if she would not be a part of Desmona's plan for John. Still, he could hardly take that hope from John, or strike Falcon from his eternal life with his soul mate—could he?

*"Lorcan, you must speak now or your wish to cancel the spell will be granted whether you intend it or not."*

"Nay…" he whispered.

*"Nay, as in, you do not desire to go through with the severance of the spell? Or nay as in, you are being defiant as usual?"*

It was no use. He loved Falcon and John too much to go through with suicide for them all. Lorcan dragged himself up and brushed the snow from his robes. He snatched up his staff and jabbed it skyward toward the cloud that now spilled heavy snowflakes upon his numb face. "Go to hell, Desmona. Your cruel spell stays. I will get through this endless torture if 'tis the last thing I ever do on this earth. And finally, one day I vow, you will be forced to give me back my body, my soul and my life."

He turned and strode away as quickly as his old, creaky bones would take him, ignoring the echo of her cackle upon the winter winds. Mentally yanking himself up by the boots, he faded into thin air and directed his mass into John's castle. He watched from a dark corner of the cave as his ever-strong charges went to work to rescue a woman who no longer seemed to fit the puzzle Lorcan had been so sure of only hours ago.

* * * * *

"Blast it to hell, where has she gone to?" John spun to face Falcon, the torch he carried casting shadows upon their faces. The humid walls of the cave's passageway glittered by the blaze of the fire, each nook and cranny alight. Yet Catriona was nowhere to be seen. Concern for her safety made John's body tremble and his thoughts jumble. His gut clenched at the thought of losing her, of never again seeing that beautiful face. To be denied the song of that lovely Scottish brogue, it saddened him deeply. It made his eyes dampen, and he could swear his heart did truly break within his chest. Ah, and just when things had begun to turn around, just when he could have sworn he had found the one woman to accept him as he was, possibly the one true love of his life.

Falcon pressed his fingers to his temples and briefly closed his eyes. "I cannot pick up her thoughts, either, my friend. We must proceed through the tunnels until we find her. Though Lance has reported that the troops have retreated, she could still be in danger...or captured," he added under his breath.

"John! Falcon!" Salena rushed into the open cavern where the men had paused to regroup. She held her skirts up off the damp, stone floor as she raced toward them. Her eyes were alight with worry and impatience. The *Centaurus* lay nestled between her breasts, its stark blue stone gleaming by the torch's flame, mirroring her eyes to exact perfection.

Althia trailed up behind Salena, her mouth twisted with distress. "Oh, forgive me, master, forgive me..." She continued to babble and mumble unintelligibly.

"'Tis Althia, she has information about Catriona," Salena supplied as she attempted to catch her breath.

John immediately turned to his maid. He gripped her upper arms and gently shook her. "Althia, 'tis all right. Please, please, calm down and relay to us what you fret about."

The woman sobbed uncontrollably, unable to get out a single lucid word. Salena offered an explanation.

"It seems a Scots soldier in the king's employ obtained entrance to the outer keep before the drawbridge was secured. He happened upon Althia in the courtyard and formed a sort of comradeship with her due to their common nationality. She unwittingly disclosed the fact that Catriona was also a Scot and currently resided here as a temporary guest. Althia was unaware the sentry sought Catriona for crimes of witchcraft against the crown."

Althia wailed, her dark head bobbing. "Me heart aches for the lass. Ah, forgive me, sir. Please forgive me. I meant the bonny lady nae harm."

"Shh, shh, we shall find her." John held her in his embrace attempting to soothe her. But his heart ached for Catriona, and his feet longed to run and seek her out.

"Oh, but nae!" She tore her tearstained face from his shoulder, her hazel eyes wide with worry. "I saw him later, I did. I watched from the upper west wing as he snatched her up outside the caste walls and whisked her away on his giant steed. I'll be tellin' ye, Lord," she said with a shudder, "he did not seem to be harmful when first we spoke. But when I gazed upon his behavior from that window, he seemed to be the epitome of evil. I do not like the looks of this a'tall."

"Aye, you may very well be right, Althia. Now tell us what you know of him." Falcon was already preparing to take flight with his soul-brother.

"Well, this was no Englishmon, I tell ye. Spoke with the verra same Scots' brogue as meself and that sweet lass, Miss Catriona. Wore the doublet, helmet and armor of James' army." Althia curled her thin upper lip. "Come to think on it now, I liken him to the verra devil!"

A lance of dread tore through John's gut as her descriptive words of the perpetrator validated his suspicions. Both Falcon and Salena groaned in unison.

"Which direction, Althia? Where has he taken her?"

"Due north, the blackguard. Forced poor Lance to lower the drawbridge before he knocked him unconscious with one swing of his fist. And God almighty, help us. Knowin' the determination and vengeance of me country's king, I fear this Duncan fellow has removed Miss Catriona to North Berwick…*to her burnin' death.*"

"Beg pardon, but did you say Duncan?" Falcon inquired, stepping closer.

Althia nodded briskly, eager to assist in any way she could. "Aye, aye. Duncan McNicol was the mon whom he claimed to be. Of the Highland clan Nicol, that I am certain of now that I think on it—by his plaid. Knew of the bloke before me departure from Edinburgh, but had never met him. Some whispered he spied for King James, and others yet gossiped of stories of seein' ghostly sightin's of him here and there followin' his burnin' execution nearly a year past. Seemed the mon made a name for hi'self from Highlands to Low as an incorrigible rogue, even durin' his marriage and his supposed 'death' period."

"The bloody bastard," John grumbled, clenching his jaw. "Althia, quickly recount this man to me once again. As descriptively as possible."

She drew a deep breath into her ample chest. The tears seemed to have dried now that she saw punishment would not be forthcoming. "Well, the mon is rather tall—nearly as tall as yerself, melord—and thin, with a sharp face structure, beady eyes and slightly crooked nose. His hair is of an auburn shade and cut severe at his jaw. As I said before, he wore the armor, helmet and doublet of a king's soldier, though his red and gold kilt proved his fealty to the clan of Nicol. He rode out on an enormous dark stallion, one that stood at least eighteen hands high, I'm thinkin'."

"I knew it!" John clenched his fists and punched the stone wall.

Salena reached for his hand and examined his knuckles. "John...nay, do not injure yourself so. She will be found."

He yanked his hand from hers. "I saw him that first moment she raced across the meadow and into my life. He sat straight and arrogant upon his steed—and the bloody murdering bastard shot her right in the lung with his own sharpened arrow. He spoke not a word. Just sat back and watched, allowing one of his men to shout orders to the soldiers in his army. He must have thought her dead with his own arrow for he and his second-in-command immediately turned and raced from the group as if his job had been seen to. Well, I say either he is a damn bad shot, or he never intended to bring her back alive to North Berwick for a trial."

John paced, his fists clenching. If he could give his own ass a swift kick this very moment, he would. His own words that day haunted him, the words that spoke of him being "Little John of none other than the League of Thieves."

*You idiot! It was Duncan McNicol whom had initially shot her. Hitting his mark, he had held back, watching as his second-in-command had ordered her to be deluged with more deadly arrows, and then he bid his men to seize her. And like some arrogant fool, you announced to him and all his cohorts who you were.*

Few knew John Lawton of Sedgewick Castle near York, and Little John of Robin Hood's nomadic band of thieves, were one and the same. But there were no doubt a select few who had found him out and might be persuaded—if the bounty was right—to reveal where one of his nearby homes were located. All Duncan had needed to do was dangle his purse in front of just the right person, and his secret identity and estate position would be known. But John swallowed his self-blame knowing full well he had not planned for her to stay so long, nor had he intended to become so enamored by her.

He recalled that moment after that passionate first kiss that had given John untold stores of power. "Then he returned and attempted to kill her once again," John went on, "after I had already healed her first fatal wound. Her very own supposedly dead husband drew back on his longbow and aimed right at his wife's lovely heart. I caught sight of him burrowing in the trees, waiting like a vulture—though at the time, I did not know his true identity. 'Twas partly why I *invisilated* here with her, to remove her to safety and finish healing her far away from this man's relentless attempts at murder. I thought she would be anonymously safe here. I thought…"

"Master, I am so verra sorry for the part I played in her abduction. He was so charmin' at first, so convincin', I—"

John saw the tears and patted her on the back. "'Tis all right, Althia. We will find her, I promise you. Go now and proceed with your household tasks. We ride and will expect a warm, cozy home upon our return. See that the cook is prepared for our foodstuff needs upon our homecoming. And please inform Chadwick his steward duties are to be set aside in favor of household watchman in my absence."

Althia nodded low and curtsied as she backed away. "Aye, master. I promise to make yer return one ye'll be rememberin' for a lifetime." She spun and followed the torchlit walls, disappearing around a bend in the tunnel's path.

John turned to face Falcon. "Brother, we ride. And if that does not lead me to her very soon, we will *invisilate* to North Berwick and head them off. Damn! If only I knew where she was at this moment, I could *invisilate* to that very location at once. I only pray to our gods that this Duncan McNicol does not choose to take her life before attempting to bring her to justice."

"I am with you, John. Let us depart at once." He swung his gaze toward his wife. "Salena, return to the safe chambers and await our return."

"Nay! I go with you."

Falcon gritted his teeth. "We do not have time to argue. Do as I say."

She lifted the *Centaurus* from her chest. "Falcon, do not be so pigheaded. This gives me immortal life just the same as you and John carry. I will be safe. Besides, you may need me and my body to replenish your powers during your journey."

"She is right, my friend," John said, already starting toward the stairs. "Allow her to travel with us."

Falcon sighed, following in John's path. "As usual, you win, woman. Now let us prepare for battle."

But Salena had already done so.

Together they made their way through the passageways and back to the castle's great hall. Quickly obtaining the needed supplies and weapons Salena had already gathered, the trio consisting of two powerful sorcerers and one woman, raced to the stables and prepared their mounts for the long, hard ride into the bitter cold of Scotland.

# Chapter Seven

ഇ

She did not know how long the journey had taken thus far. They had ridden directly into the oncoming storm cloud. Blustery winds carried with it the heavy flakes of a near-blizzard. The snow deepened, and yet Duncan forced the Friesian through the drifts, onward toward Scotland and her execution. Catriona had long since lost feeling in her feet and hands, which Duncan had opted to bind following her many efforts to bolt from his mount. She groaned inwardly, attempting to muffle her discomfort. Nay, she did not wish to give the bastard the satisfaction of witnessing her pain and distress.

The day's inclement weather gave way to the still of dusk, and in turn, dusk to the dead of night. Catriona stared at the trudging rhythm of the hooves as the steed continued his nonstop journey. How grateful she was that she had not taken time to remove her long tresses from inside her cloak after donning it in the cave. Her hair could have easily gotten entangled in the horse's legs as Duncan urged him on…and mayhap have every strand ripped from her scalp by now. Or she could have been trampled and dead this very moment!

She tried to put the frightening thoughts from her mind, to keep her head clear so she could plan a possible escape. But the muffled drone of the hoofbeats trudging through the deep snow reverberated in her ears. Her temples ached due to the prone position Duncan had strung her in, tossed across his lap like a sack of dead prey. Blood pounded incessantly in her brain while white stars burst before her vision. The pommel of the saddle poked her side time and time again as the stallion rocked and lurched in his lumbered flight.

Tears of humiliation and anger filled her eyes. So she focused on the one saving grace she had, the warmth of the horse's hide against her front side. Forcing the tears to dry, she thought of John. She longed to be in his arms again, to watch the passion build in his liquid-blue eyes. Her heart ached for him, yearned to know if he had come after her or simply shrugged his shoulders at her sudden escape. Did he even know Duncan and his sentries had been the ones Lance had announced as lurking outside the keep? Nay, not unless the men Duncan had left behind had been detained and questioned by John and the few men John had remaining on his grounds. Duncan's small army had not come with them, but she prayed they had gone on and left Sedgewick Castle unscathed. Oh, how she hoped Duncan had not furthered his revenge by ordering undue mayhem upon John's household and staff!

*Stop it, Catriona, just stop it now!* She would drive herself to daftness if she continued to wish John had come after her, or to worry over what deaths she may have caused. Instead, she forced herself to think of something soothing. Her thoughts drifted to his home, its comfort and stately beauty.

But she did not think of it for long. The horse suddenly shifted, nearly dumping her from its high back. Challenged now, the mount was jostled to the side in an attempt to avoid the abrupt change of terrain. The land rose from snow-blanketed rolling hills into deep gorges and patches of rocky crags jutting up at random intervals in the vast space ahead. If the horse jolted one more time, Catriona feared she would either break her neck or become incontinent of her fluid wastes. Her lower abdomen ached for relief. She tightened her body attempting to hold on, but she worried the pressure against her stomach may cause her to lose control. Basic animal needs plagued her, the hunger for food and water, the drive to seek warmth, comfort and sleep—to simply survive. She licked her parched lips, longing for a flagon of cool water and a single jerky of beef. But still, Duncan pushed on heedless to her discomfort.

She had since given up on pleading with him to, at the very least, provide her basic comforts. Instead she thought to use logic, firmness and manipulation. "Halt this horse at once, Duncan."

He yanked upward on the hood of her cape. "Ah, the witch speaks once again—but not for long. Now silence, I say. I'll be stoppin' when I've a mind to do so, and not one minute before that, ye hear?"

"For God's sake, ye bastard," she rasped, fighting for breath due to the choking garment, "I need to...relieve meself."

He snorted. "And who would be keepin' ye from doin' so?"

"So ye'd be havin' me to wet yer precious steed? Fine. Then I'll be stinkin' the horse's hide, along with yer own bloody garments."

"Nae!" Duncan stiffened and released the cape. "Now that ye be puttin' it that way..."

He guided the stallion toward an overhang jutting from one wall of the gorge. The ground appeared rocky and dry beneath, void of the snow that blanketed the remainder of the earth. Dismounting just outside its perimeter, Duncan dragged her from the horse's back and set her in the snow. Her ankles were so very sore, she almost welcomed the bite of the cold against her lower legs. It took a long moment for the blood to move through her numb body, but bless the dead spirits, it felt like heaven to be on solid, unmoving ground again!

"Well?" By the light of the moon, she could see his narrowed eyes, the deadly impatience.

"Well?" she echoed, holding up her arms. "Are ye daft? By a witch's brew—"

"Do not speak of witches, I tell ye!" His lanky body trembled while his voice reverberated through the glen. The odor of his rank breath blasted in her face and made her want to retch.

She leaned back, expecting a slap that did not come. "And I ask ye, how in the bloody hell do ye expect me to take care of me business without ye takin' these farthin' ties off me wrists and ankles first?"

He paused, his gaze sliding downward. "Eh, Christ," he sighed in moody resignation. "Hell, as long as we're stopped and ye're untied, we might as well make camp here." Duncan unfastened the knots as he spoke, his tone grumpy and somewhat wary. "But I warn ye, Catriona, do not give me any reason to draw me dirk and see it settled between yer breasts."

Nay, she was no fool. John was not here to heal her wounds and save her life. "Ye can bet I'll be heedin' yer advice, blackguard, for I wish to live—and I will, at that." Despite the conviction in her voice, fear ate away at her stomach.

"Aye," he said with a snicker. "Ye'll live all right...up 'til I secure ye to yer witch's stake in North Berwick and light the fire beneath ye. Under the king's approvin' stare, ye see."

"We'll be seein' about that, *dear* husband." Flexing her stiff hands and arms, she spun on her heels and, with a wobbly gait, made her way to a nearby bush. Attempting escape crossed her mind, but Duncan followed, standing guard as she relieved herself. And while the thought of his vile stare upon her flesh made her skin crawl, she was beyond caring. Despite the biting cold that nipped at her rear, the respite that flooded her body and her abdomen made her grateful he had given her this small reprieve. Perhaps it would be her last?

As she trudged back to the snow-free, protective overhang, curiosity nagged at her. It wended its way into a plan...

"In the months followin' yer 'death', why did ye wait so long to come after me, Duncan? Why did ye not just haul me in durin' our marriage when we cohabited together?"

He pulled the saddle from the horse's back and set it in the dry area beneath the jutting rock designated as their campsite. As he spoke, she followed him around a small cluster of trees set near the rocky space, assisting in the gathering of kindling. Catriona longed for the heat of a fire enough to join forces with him in this task.

"Didn't we already go through this when I found ye at the bloke's castle?"

She sighed. "So we did. But would ye care to enlighten me once again? I find it all so verra astonishin' — not to mention maddenin' — that ye pulled it off," she added in an attempt to feed his ego.

He roared with heinous laughter and took the bait. "Verra well, wench. Three verra good reasons come to mind," he said conversationally as he bent to pluck up several small twigs and broken logs. "First, I needed to gain access to yer Gypsy village without bein' seen as an outsider or suspected of anythin' but a mon smitten with one of their own. 'Twas imperative to weedin' out the wickedness within yer band of witches. See, I had to do this to distinguish between the innocent folk and those deservin' to burn for their crimes — not that I gave a fuckin' hell about the innocent. But the king wished to go about it methodically so as not to spur an uprisin' from the Scots. 'Course, I'm sure ye'll be askin' me, 'twould have been much faster and easier to just burn the whole filthy place down, wouldn't it?"

Catriona gritted her teeth. She leaned down and spied a clump of dried sticks behind a small boulder set between the edge of their dry camp area and the trees. "So, to be gettin' in the good graces of all of me people, ye wooed and married me, wastin' away a naïve maid's virginity with yer deceitful façade."

"Oh, nae," he returned with a vile grin as he strode under the ledge and squatted to arrange the wood. Duncan licked his thin lips, his gaze moving lower to assess her body's length. It made her stomach roil and pinpricks of fear shimmied up her spine. "There be nae waste to the delights of a Gypsy tramp...when one is in the mood for it."

She ignored the innuendo and dropped the small stack of limbs on his pile. "And the second reason would be?"

Duncan fetched a small tinderbox from the saddlebag and bent his head to the task of lighting the fire. "Why, riches, of course. The king is a verra generous mon to those who fight against evil in his name."

"Of course. Greed. I perfectly understand that in light of the new Duncan McNicol." The flames of the campfire suddenly ignited making Catriona flinch. "But then there is yer final reason..."

"Aye." Crouching, he rubbed his hands together over the small bonfire, a selfish man seeking the very fire he sets upon others to die by. "I needed to present the king with evidence of yer ability to speak to the dead. Ye had yet to reveal such a wicked ceremony to me, and I was loath to throw ye upon the king's mercy without first knowin' for certain if ye truly were a witch. Now see, the king specifically demanded that once I had yer...talent confirmed, I was to lug ye to court so he could speak to his own dead loved ones—that is, before he had ye burned at the stake."

*Ah, so the plot coagulates.* The hypocritical king wanted to enlist her services before presenting her to his kingdom as a convicted witch and burning her to death. Luckily, she had been self-conscious and had hesitated in revealing her skills to her husband. She had not wished to share her "abnormality" with him before she was ready.

His candid honesty led her into the final part of her plan. "Well, would ye like to confirm me 'talent' now, Duncan?"

He blinked, clearly shocked by her question. "What did ye say?"

"I repeat, before ye throw me upon the king's mercy, wouldn't ye like to confirm me talents now, to be certain of me transgressions? I could perform a séance for ye right here and now. In fact, I could assist ye in talkin' to...Fraser."

Duncan gasped and fell back onto his hands. "F-Fraser? D-did ye say, Fraser?"

Though she was dying to seek the warmth of the blaze, she assembled her own heat by narrowing her eyes, crossing her arms and leaning over him. "Aye, I said Fraser. He came to me a time or two durin' our marriage askin' to come through to ye. But I did not allow it, didn't kent for sure who he was."

"Y-ye *are* a witch!" He crumbled backward onto his elbows, his beady eyes glittering by the firelight, revealing his sudden fear and trepidation. He stared agog at her as if she were some sort of abominable monster.

"If that is what ye and yer king wish to call it, then aye, I am a witch."

"T-tell me, what did he say to ye? Is he all right? Does he…miss me?"

Though she had had her suspicions, she had not the faintest inkling whom this Fraser had been. Strangely, he had struggled to come through during one of her séances she had kept hidden from Duncan during their short marriage. But he had made himself known as an acquaintance of Duncan's, and had begged to be channeled through to speak to him. There had been a sense of pain, desperation, perhaps love and possibly anger coming across within his spirit. In fact, who or what he really was in relation to Duncan did not come full circle until this very moment, until she actually *heard* Duncan's words coupled with the sappy hope alight in his eyes.

"So, this Fraser was yer former lover, eh?"

He swallowed audibly, the large knot in his throat bobbing up and down. "He was me footmon. Died three year's past."

Catriona leaned closer. "All right then, yer footmon. But he was also yer lover, wasn't he, Duncan?"

She nearly gasped when tears filled his eyes. His gaze fell to stare into the leaping flames. "Aye."

"So all that fumblin' passion in our bed, 'twas a farce?" She compared John to Duncan. But there was just no comparison between Duncan's attempts at rutting and John's perfection in lovemaking.

Duncan managed to soak her with an angry glare. "Nae, I...I have a penchant for..."

When he did not finish, she took a guess. "For both male and female?"

There were no words to that, just a curt nod and the very first wash of embarrassment she had ever seen cross his face.

Images of herself kissing Salena while John pummeled her from behind filled her thoughts. "I...days ago, I would not have understood it, but tonight, I think I can comprehend it to a degree. Now, let us get on with it. I ask ye most sincerely, would ye like to speak with him, or nae?" She straightened to a standing position, her back erect, her arms crossed over her flapping cloak.

"Can I?" Glee shone across the sharp features of his face.

If he were not such a vindictive, hypocritical ass, Catriona's heart would have bled for him. But it would behoove her to remember all the pain and destruction he had caused. He had killed his own twin brother for his greedy purposes, to further a plan to remain in the king's good graces to partake of his royal coffers. And foremost, Duncan had masqueraded as an innocent who had secretly had her beloved mother burned to death, along with several others in her village. Oh yes, she only had to recall the putrid odor of burning bodies to remember what a monster this man truly was.

She shrugged nonchalantly, though she prayed he would succumb to temptation and play into her plan. "'Tis yer choice. I can bring him through without a bit of a problem, that I am certain of. But if ye do not wish to..."

"Nae, I do, I do!"

She hesitated long enough to draw out the drama. "All right, then. But only on one condition…"

His lips thinned. "Should have known there would be a catch. What would Yer Royal Witch Highness like?"

"I am thirsty and hungry. And I will need to warm me bones before any spirits can channel through me."

\* \* \* \* \*

Warm, dry and fed now, Catriona sat cross-legged on the parched stone floor below the rocky overhang. Duncan sat facing her in the same manner. With the fire at her left, she swallowed her revulsion and clasped his hands.

"Ye must close yer eyes 'til I give ye permission to open them."

Duncan sent her a wary look, but obeyed, nonetheless. "Just get on with it," he grumbled.

The snow had ceased falling, but the winds continued to whistle eerie and low through the gorge. Night had descended moonless and black, its inky nothingness—like her dream with Lorcan and Duncan—spilling out across the craggy glen and encroaching on the glow of their campfire. An owl hooted in the distance, its mournful call resonating across the barren lands. A pair of foxes skittered through the snow on the outer edges of camp enticed by the glow of flames and the scent of a possible food source. Catriona inhaled the odor of acrid smoke mixed with that of Duncan's perspiration. Though inexplicable or even spine-chilling at times, the ambiance and all the things surrounding her were conducive to bringing forth spirits. She also needed access to the smells and moods of those people— namely Duncan at present—who sought loved ones in order to lure the spirits into this dimension and bring them into present being. And most times, she required the dark of night and the songs of nature in order to concentrate and perform as the medium.

Catriona drew in a long cleansing breath, released it. "Oh spirits in the other realm, hear me call…"

Silence followed for a full moment. The winds burst in, blowing the cloak's hood from her head, ruffling her hair. She focused on a distant point above Duncan's head. The usual vibrations started, almost imperceptible at first, but gradually increasing until her body trembled uncontrollably.

"What the hell…" Duncan opened his eyes and pulled back, struggling to remove his hands from hers.

She held tight and snapped, "Do not move! Ye must remain quiet, still and keep yer eyes closed 'til I tell ye otherwise, or the séance could be aborted."

His gaze shone like wide mouse eyes cornered by the cat, yet still ogling the cheese. "This is crazy, bizarre. Y-ye're scarin' me."

"Do ye want to speak with yer lover Fraser or nae?"

"Well, of course I do, but—"

"Then hush!"

His nostrils flared, and for the briefest moment, Catriona feared she had pushed him too far. But after an instant of settling in again and tightening his big hands around her small ones, his eyes fluttered shut.

"Oh spirits in the other realm, hear me call," she repeated.

The breeze increased in velocity and swirled around the camp. It caused the flames to dance and sputter. Ashes rose and drifted hither and yon into the black of night. The tremors she always dreaded resumed with a vengeance.

"Any and all dead, ye are not welcome unless called forth by name." A low, distant moan of protests sounded, as if she listened to an angry crowd of spirits from afar.

Duncan drew in a hiss of fear and clamped his eyelids tightly shut. A thin line of sweat dribbled down his temple and made a wet, vertical path to his jaw.

"Chosen soul, I give ye consent to speak through and to communicate with Duncan upon his request." She inhaled and went on with her initial connections. "Duncan McNicol of the clan Nicol, I now give ye bid to make yer request. Call out the name of the spirit ye wish to contact."

He gulped audibly. "F-Fraser Douglas? Are ye there?"

The wind whistled in high-pitched tones. Snow whirled up into a conical shape around Duncan. The shuddering ceased all at once. Catriona glanced to her left, just above the flames, to see the misty spirit materialize, that of a small thin man, fair of hair with round blue eyes. He was what she would call pretty, almost effeminate upon very first sight. But all-male anger blazed in the depths of those gorgeous eyes.

"*Aye, I am here, Duncan.*" His likeness hovered, rippling through the rising heat of the fire.

Duncan gasped at the familiar voice. He rocked from side to side, gripping Catriona's hands almost painfully. "Oh, God. Is it really ye? Is it true?"

"'Tis true," Catriona replied. "Ye can open yer eyes now."

His lids fluttered open and he drew in a sharp breath when his gaze found Fraser's apparition. One lone tear pooled in the corner of his left eye. "Fraser! Holy hell, 'tis truly ye."

"*Mmm, in the spirit flesh…thanks to ye.*"

"Nae, I do not ken what ye're—nae!"

"*Ah, but ye do, me deceitful lover, ye do. God help me, how I have longed to come through to ye. I called upon yer wife here many a time after yer blasted farce of a weddin'. Though I did not supply her with details, she refused to believe me impassioned pleas to haunt ye, chose to ignore the desperation in me soul. Oh, I cannot blame her, mind ye, but mon, do ye ken how good it feels to finally be able to speak me heart to ye?*"

"Oh, aye, aye, please speak yer heart! I have so missed ye too. I have—"

"*Ye missed me?*" He spat it with conviction and a scathing, shrill tone. "*Ha! Ye bloody bastard!*"

Duncan let out a squeal of shock and tried to disentangle his hands from hers.

"Duncan, stop at once! Ye must continue to hold me hands. Farthin' hell, do ye wish to terminate the connection?" she asked, squeezing his fingers with every ounce of her strength.

*"Ye fuckin' bastard! Ye had me burned to a crisp. And due to me hatred for ye, I remain prisoner within a dead mon's purgatory. But ye put me through hell, through the most unbearable pain I have ever endured. The horror of yer betrayal still haunts me, still burns me verra soul, even in death. Ye have driven me into this purgatory because of this blasted resentment I cannot rid meself of. God, how I've longed to just choke the verra life from yer fuckin' neck!"*

"Nae…" Duncan rose up on his knees, his hands gripping Catriona's, even as he trembled. His eyes beheld Fraser's image, beseeching him as the tears rolled off his cheeks and onto his cloak. "Fraser, love, I am so verra sorry. I beg of ye, forgive me, please. 'Twas the king. H-he insisted ye were bad for me, swore ye were a spawn of the devil, a true sorcerer for capturin' me heart and causin' me to neglect and shirk me witch-hunting duties. Please ken, it tore me soul out of me chest to order the fire lit, to see ye strung up there like a piece of meat to be roasted. See, 'twas James…I did it at James' command, else face me own execution."

*"And now ye shall face Satan in hell…"*

"Nae!" He screamed it, his cry reverberating off the canyon walls. Duncan came to his feet dragging her with him.

"Duncan," Catriona warned through clenched teeth, "ye must calm down or we will lose him."

His rabid gaze flicked down to her. "Ye did this, didn't ye? I fell under yer witch's spell yet again and allowed ye to conjure up this fraudulent image of me beloved Fraser."

She shook her head frantically, a sudden stab of fear twisting in her gut. "Nae, I swear, 'tis real, 'tis yer Fraser in the verra spirit flesh. I merely brought him through to ye."

"*Do not do this, Duncan. Ye ken 'tis me. Face yer sins, ye bastard, or die in hell. Ye owe me yer sincere oath of repentance, though I cannot see how ye will ever be worthy of forgiveness. Nonetheless, if I receive it, I can then begin to forgive ye, and be delivered into heaven, as it should be.*"

Duncan jerked his chin up and narrowed his eyes. "Silence!" To Catriona, he growled, "Ye bitch. Ye had me fooled for a time, but nae more."

"Nae, do not—"

Duncan jerked his hands from hers and Fraser's roar of angered objection snapped off, as if Duncan had slammed a lid onto a roiling pot of brew. Fraser's spirit dissipated into the rising smoke of the fire. The remaining vibrations Catriona had begun to experience again ceased all at once.

"To hell with the riches the king promised me for bringin' ye unto him. Ye must die this instant!"

"Duncan, nae, ye cannot—"

The slap cracked across her cheek with such force, she fell to the rocky floor of their camp. Her heated gaze rose to snare him with as much hate as she could muster over the throbbing pain in her jaw. "Ye fuckin' bastard!"

He reached down and yanked her to her feet. "Better a bastard than a harlot witch of the devil."

Anger overrode the terror of what she knew he had planned for her in the minutes ahead. She spat in his face.

After a long moment of stunned disbelief, he spat back, and the warm, vile-smelling moisture dribbling down her cheek made her stomach churn.

"It sickens me to think I lay with ye in the same bed," she hissed, swiping the spittle with her sleeve. "Talk of the devil. Ye are the epitome of all things vile and revoltin'."

Duncan swept her with a look of his own revulsion. "Yer wicked charms...aye, ye'll be payin' Satan for all yer transgressions, ye bloody whore."

Catriona knew he meant she would die this night. She would never see John again, never feel his arms around her or his gentle, loving touch upon her flesh. Tears filled her eyes, but she refused to allow them to spill over.

"I'll be thinkin' we shall see who pays, Duncan. We shall see..."

"Nae more, witch. I forfeit the king's payment in favor of extinguishin' ye this night. Ye must pay for all yer wicked indiscretions, and pay now."

He reached down, snatched up the saddlebag and dragged her out into the snow. His fingers bit into her upper arm. Leaning back against his powerful hold, she dropped her head back, screaming into the dark of night with all the strength she could draw from her lungs. It rent the air with a mournful, horror-filled tune. She heard the skittish flight of a bird as it flew off in fear of the sudden commotion. A rabbit scurried away seeking escape from the falsely perceived hunter. Duncan ignored her attempts at kicking, and warded off her flailing, free arm with little effort.

A chilly blast of air shot up her cloak, but it was the path he took her on that made her shiver. Toward the lone dead yew tree standing tall and broken in the valley of the gorge. Black against black, save for the flicker of firelight, it swayed in the winds as if mocking her.

"Nae..." She choked it out, longing to muster the bravery to march defiant and proud up the path he laid for her. But she did not wish to die! Images of John's handsome face flashed through her mind.

"Oh, aye." He sniggered, the sound coming out fiendish and crazed. "Time for the sorceress to die."

As he plucked her up and curled one arm around her waist, holding her body tight and angled painfully to his hip, he dropped the saddlebag and kicked it open. A huge looping of rope fell out onto the snow. Her eyes widened, each action he took seeming to shove her closer to death's door.

*I do not wish to die! John, John, me honorable, chivalrous bandit Little John, where are ye?*

But she knew he would not come. How could he? He would have no way of knowing her location, and what's more, he had no reason to seek her out after she had fled the safe haven he offered her. Panic flooded her chest making her heartbeat crash into her breastbone and well up into her throat. The pulse of it reverberated in her ears like a relentless, pounding surf. She flailed, kicked, bit, screamed and watched with maddening despair as her long hair became the only part of her that proved able to escape him. It fell down in waves, streaming over his legs, flapping in the breeze like a flag of surrender.

"Duncan, ye cannot do this to me. I am yer wife, for Christ's sake. Ye cannot murder yer own wife."

"Wife?" he croaked, drawing back to punch her even as he continued to hold her hostage. She dodged the blow somewhat, managing to deflect it to her jaw rather than her eye, but nonetheless, she still saw stars. "A witch—who plots against the king, commits adultery against her husband, casts hedonistic spells upon every person in her wake—cannot be a true wife."

With a brutish growl, he threw her into the barren tree trunk restraining her body with his, and stretched a loop of rope across her neck. Catriona struggled for every breath. Dots blinked before her vision. She looked into his crazed eyes, silently begged him to release the constraint just enough to draw one more breath. But he refused. His face reddened in the waning light of the fire as he held his own breath, tightening his hold. Catriona gripped his hands, pulling, scratching, squeezing, but he did not budge. She felt the bite of rope into her flesh, fought the outer clutches of unconsciousness...of death.

Frantic now for air and blessed life, the instinct to survive jolting through her brain, she kneed him. But he protected his balls by kicking her shin just before she made contact. The sickening crack she heard mimicked that of a snapping twig. She screamed again, this time a strangled, snarling sound of hopelessness and anguish. Pain shattered in her leg and she knew at that second that he had broken her bone. Instant nausea swirled in her gut and she struggled to fend off the clutches of oblivion. No longer able to focus on the strength of escape, she reached behind her to cling to the tree, to avoid sliding down and having to put weight on the injured leg if he should suddenly release her.

And he did free her at the very second the thought had entered her mind. But freedom came brief and cruel. Before she realized what he had done, before she could drag two full breaths into her burning lungs, he had her pinioned to the tree again. Duncan wound the rope around and around her torso and the tree trunk. He secured it so snugly she could barely draw half a breath into her lungs. Ah, but by the grace of God, he had lowered it, and not encircled it around her neck.

"Duncan," she rasped, her throat now scratchy and raw. "Please do not do this…please, I beg of ye."

He shot her a murderous glower and crossed to their campfire, carefully choosing kindling and an armload of several thicker branches. Next he ambled over and arranged them at her feet. Duncan finally knelt and drew out the tinderbox.

"Nae one, not even a spawn of the devil himself," he swore, his teeth clenched, "will ever use me Fraser against me as ye just now did. Ye made it all up with yer malicious witchcraft."

"Nae, 'twas him, I swear it! I did not conjure it up. I merely brought his spirit forth for ye to speak with just as ye requested. Duncan, ye must take heart. Seems ye murdered yer own lover, and he remains angered in death, as he should. 'Tis nae true that I invented it! Duncan, please *did not*—"

"Liar! Silence, I say, or I'll be burnin' down yer whole village without allowin' so much as a single minute of a trial for any of them."

With the flint, he struck a sharp blow against the fire steel. A shower of red sparks fell onto the tinder, and he quickly held a sulfur match to the embers in order to ignite the fire. Smoke rose as it caught to first the kindling then to the hem of her cloak. Instant heat permeated the layers of her clothing and slowly soaked into her flesh. The flames rose higher, catching to the twigs, licking at her braies and boots beneath.

Duncan stepped back and watched, his eyes gleaming with vindictive hatred. "Finally ye'll be goin' to hell where ye belong, ye evil witch." He spun, turning his back on her, and returned to the camp. Even though she screamed, even though she cried and wailed and bucked away from the searing pain when the flames finally caught to her braies and engulfed her, he lay down upon a blanket next to the campfire and watched his wife burn.

Catriona howled and writhed against the searing heat, never having felt such intense pain in all of her life. As delirium overtook her and the pungent odor of burning flesh and hair filled her nostrils, all those who had gone before her flashed in her mind…Duncan's poor, unsuspecting brother, several of her Gypsy kin, the many spirits she had channeled through to the living, her dear, sweet ma.

All she could do now was beg for swift death. As she did so, even as she convulsed in pain and prayed to God for forgiveness and mercy on her soul, she thought of one more person. Catriona cried out his name just before she toppled into blackness.

"*John!*"

# Chapter Eight

80

"I smell something...smoke," Salena murmured on a sniff.

Falcon shook his head. "I tell you, John, she has always had the snout of a bloodhound. Can smell the food before the cook even thinks to prepare it."

"This is no time to jest," John said under his breath to Falcon. To Salena, he asked with impatience, "Can you tell what direction it comes from?"

She nodded, whirling her mount toward his. "Due north-northwest. And I also—oh, what was that? Was that a scream?"

John perked his ears. Yes, he thought he heard what sounded like a second cry of a bobcat, yet it held an almost gravelly form of Catriona's voice in it. "Falcon, is she close enough? Can you pick up her location by her thoughts?"

Falcon narrowed his eyes and scanned the rocky horizon. "Nay, nothing. Must be too far away," he mumbled on a sigh. The opening of a gorge lay ahead as he searched toward the sound of the screams. He started to rein his horse around westward when it appeared something had caught his eye to the north. "What is that? A flicker upon the canyon walls."

"A flicker?"

"Yes..." Falcon urged his mount closer. "Ah, there, do you see it? There must be a fire up ahead."

"Dismount at once!" John ordered.

Salena and Falcon had been with John for what seemed forever. There was no need for Falcon to read John's mind, or for Salena to inquire as to the purpose of his sudden demand.

They both obeyed him without further delay and leapt to the snow-packed ground. Racing up to John's side, they hooked their arms around his waist, one on each side of him.

Now that John knew the location he sought, he could *invisilate* with accuracy. He wrapped his arms around them and shouted, "Core of my magic, supreme and so sure, follow the screams and transport us to her."

The sharp suction of the vortex drew on them. John closed his eyes as a portion of his energy was sapped from his soul. Within two seconds, they appeared by the fire. What met his eyes made him dizzy with both shock and anger. Her charred lower body thrashed and fought against the ropes that bound her to the tree trunk. Her cloak ignited into an inferno that nipped at the ends of her unbound hair. John smelled the sharp odor of both burning tresses and flesh. He would never forget the pain-racked screams, the horror on her scorched face and the far-away glaze in her lovely eyes.

"*Nay!*" His own cry rent the night air, frightening the wildlife away. Without a moment's pause, he drew on his powers and raced in a lightning-quick circle around her. It achieved just what he hoped it would. The snow flew up, smothering the flames and coating her burned body with its cool, numbing quality. In the wake of the speedy action, all that remained of the fire was the sizzle of wet wood and the plumes of smoke.

The arrow hit John square in the back. He neither felt the pain nor the anger that simmered there, for he knew where the arrow had come from. Duncan. But his only concern at the moment was for Catriona. There was no doubt Falcon and Salena would see to Duncan. John broke off the tip that had penetrated his abdomen, and reached behind himself. He yanked out the arrow with a grunt, tossing it aside. Grasping the dagger at his waist, he stepped up to Catriona. She hung slumped from the tree, her whole person smoking, her body blackened from the chest down.

Love and panic warred in his mind. He sliced at the burnt ropes cutting them away from her with adept speed. His jaw clenched with rage and helplessness, and he felt the tears well up in his eyes. God help him, but she appeared to be dead! Had he been minutes too late? All those extraordinary powers at the disposal of he and Falcon, and he had not been able to perform the miracle of saving her in time? Through all the snow, smoke, charred remnants of her clothing and the sickening singe of flesh, he could not discern for sure if she lived. He refused to think what it would mean if he had been delayed too long.

His gut churned with nausea and regret. "Catriona...Catriona, please, *please*, my love, awaken. 'Tis John."

She stirred and he let out a moan of relief ridden on a sigh. Strangled groans of pain tore from her smoke-drenched lungs. As he continued to carefully but swiftly free her, out of the corner of his eye he detected the rise and fall of her chest. Her head lolled and rolled in a circle around her shoulders, the singed ends of her hair brushing her reddened shoulders and chest. Even as he cut her free, he heard the commotion behind him, Duncan's shouts, Falcon's stern warnings. But John had only one goal, one new purpose in life.

Catriona and her rescue and healing.

He peeled the crispy bindings away and caught her in his arms. With as much care as he could render while carrying out the task with rapid adeptness, John cradled her in his embrace and knelt in the snow. The scorched odors assailed his nostrils, and it reminded him he had never felt such hatred for any human being as he did at this moment for her husband. This Duncan would pay with his life if John had anything to say about it—but first he must heal her and take away all the pain the bastard had caused her.

Catriona's eyelids fluttered open, the tips of the lashes singed. She coughed and wheezed, attempting to draw air through the damaged passageway of her windpipe. He watched as the green orbs found and focused on him, a look of disbelief in their depths.

"John…" she said with a hoarse, whisper-soft voice. "Is that ye? Am I in heaven?"

"Aye, 'tis me. And no, my love, you are not in heaven. But you are going to be fine." *I pray it is so!* "Just lie still for me."

"John…oh, how it hurts! P-please just let me die. Please, so the pain will end."

"Nay! I will not let you die! Shh, hold still. You know I am capable of healing you. Just try to relax, sweetheart. Hold on to life — please! I beg of you, do not leave me."

The clutches of unconsciousness assailed her on a long moan of anguish. He held his breath, his eyes widening, until he was assured air passed through her lungs.

Drawing in a deep breath, he gathered his forces, centering it in the palms of his hands. John knew this would sap his energy far more than healing her arrow wounds had that first day. He could only hope that the foursome she had shared with him, Falcon and Salena, had been enough to sustain John to perform the extensive lifesaving measures needed.

He started with her chest, carefully peeling away what remained of garments as he went. He knew she required air first and foremost to live, so he began with her lungs. The hot-cold vibrations shot through his arms with little effort. He centered each palm over a breast and rubbed in a circular motion, closing his eyes until he felt the positive force of healthy tissue being transmitted back to him. He moved up to her neck, healing both the reddened flesh and her damaged air passage. Relief flooded his system when her ragged, distressed respirations were gradually restored to soft, slow breaths.

Next he moved to her face feeling the slight lessening of his own strength. He rubbed his hands over her scalded skin, fluids seeping out as the raised blisters tore. His breath nearly caught in his throat at the startling beauty that slowly returned, as if he had drawn a damaged drape away from her face and let the breathtaking sunlight shine through.

Slight dizziness now warbled through his head as he taxed himself, moving down her arms, abdomen and thighs, again peeling away the remnants of burnt clothing as he worked.

"Holy mother of hell!" he bit out when he finally reached her right shin. Blackened flesh had been melded to the sharp jut of snapped bone. "The bastard broke her leg."

John glanced across the small clearing of the gorge and narrowed his gaze on Duncan who now stood backed against the canyon wall as Falcon gave him a tongue-lashing. Rage built to a maddening level. It boiled inside him making him long to go crush that asshole's neck and take his very life from him. But Catriona lay unconscious and unfeeling at the moment, and he did not wish her to suffer even one iota of pain once she awoke.

Gathering his energy and focus once again, he concentrated on curing her ailment. It took quite a bit more power than he had anticipated, but he focused, determined to repair the fractured bone. And he did. The leg straightened, and he felt the energy of healed bone and renewed skin transmit into his hands. Fighting the fatigue and dizziness, he moved down her opposite leg and foot, repairing every cell. He then rolled her over and inspected her backside. Only when the last area of flesh had been restored to its normal dusky tint and silken texture did John collapse in the snow and curl his body behind hers.

Spent, his skin beading with sweat, he drew her close and stared over her body toward the commotion across the gully. Now that his attention could be drawn away from her, he could hear every word being spoken, but his body had not the energy to rise.

"I say there, sorry chap, you best re-sheath your dirk, or face death."

"Nae!" Duncan growled, jutting the sharp weapon at Falcon. He easily dodged the swipe and leapt to Duncan's left. But Duncan's eyes widened and he gasped when he glanced across the craggy ground and saw Catriona lying unscathed but unconscious, tucked lovingly into the crook of John's body. "Witches! All of ye are witches. Ye will all die in the name of King James of Scotland."

"Salena," Falcon murmured, never taking his eyes from the crazed man. "Go to them at once. Get out of this madman's reach."

She jutted her chin and furrowed her brow, swinging her gaze to her husband. "Not a chance. Not until this fool is taken care of. Catriona is now well, and John will simply need revitalizing."

"Do not be stubborn, woman! Remember the uncertainty of the amulet…" He lashed out at her verbally, John knew, due to his worry over her welfare. If the pendant should be accidentally—or intentionally—removed from around her neck, there would be no immediate way of knowing what it could mean for her. It was unknown if its temporary immortal qualities would lift and instantaneously thrust swift death upon her, or if she would be safe long enough to place the protective *Centaurus* back around her neck. But no one had ever wished to test its boundaries to be certain, therefore Salena had never removed it.

"Stubborn? I love you with all of my life, husband! But 'tis you who remains obstinate throughout the decades, striving to continually protect me from—"

"Salena, look out!" John shouted weakly.

During the distraction of the marital disagreement, Duncan had turned the tables. He now detained Salena with his forearm across her breasts and her back held against his chest. With the other hand, he positioned the blade of his basket-hilted sword across her neck.

"Fools, all of ye!" Duncan hissed. "Now, ye bastard Robin Hood, either ye go and fetch me mount, or I'll be slittin' yer pretty little wife's throat. Hmm," he added glancing over her shoulder at the *Centaurus* nestled between the swell of bosom. "And I believe I'll help meself to that rich jewel danglin' about her neck, as well."

"Get your bloody, filthy hands off her this instant!" Falcon's fists were clenched, as were his teeth. A murderous gleam shone in his eyes. He took two strides, starting toward Duncan.

"Uh-uh-uh, ye come any closer, ye thievin' bandit, and ye can bet I'll be slicin' this gorgeous head right off her slim shoulders."

Falcon stopped dead in his path. John knew why he hesitated. They dare not experiment with the *Centaurus'* powers until absolutely necessary. And Falcon knew John would be of no help, for he currently had drained all his healing stores until further rejuvenation.

Duncan cackled, sounding much like the witches he relentlessly pursued. To prove his point and determination at escape, he dragged the blade across her throat. A thin line of blood trickled down her slim, pale throat. Salena gasped, stiffening at the sharp pain, but she did not attempt to take flight. She stared wide-eyed and fearful at Falcon, suddenly aware it seemed, of her true vulnerability for the first time since donning the *Centaurus*.

"I swear, if you draw one more drop of blood from her veins, you are a dead man."

"Ah, standin' there like a coward, ye are, shootin' empty threats and leavin' yer poor wife in me great company." Duncan snickered, his eyes glazing with the intoxication of control. "And here I was thinkin' ye were some kind of brave, legendary hero or somethin'. Why, ye ain't nothin' but a spineless, bloody bastard!"

With that last word, Duncan's voice rose to a manic, high-pitched tone. His guffaw echoed, bouncing over the stone rocks and walls. Apparently, though, he was not yet done with his taunting tirade.

"Just look at ye." He swiped the sword deeper, eliciting a strangled scream from Salena. Falcon swore and crouched in a stance, poised to attack at that very second. "What happened to yer supposed love for her, ye fuckin' —"

But before Duncan could finish the statement, his rant ended abruptly. The arrow struck him clean through the right side of his chest. His eyes snapped in surprise. He looked down to find himself speared side-to-side, the arrow having passed between his ribs and into his heart and lungs. The shocked gaze followed the direction of where the arrow had come from, resting upon his assailant, Little John. Duncan stumbled backward, releasing Salena in favor of catching his own body before it hit the ground with a thud. His breaths tore ragged and gurgled from his throat. Blood shot out from wound and mouth, spattering the rock and snow. The deep red splotches against stark white shone almost black in the waning firelight. He collapsed to the earth in a thrashing heap.

Falcon captured Salena in his embrace and dragged her toward John and Catriona. "Lorcan alive, if you ever disobey me like that again, I'll..." He forced her face into his chest, watching with a satisfied glare as Duncan writhed and fought for his last breaths of life.

"Fraser..." Duncan moaned aloud. "Fraser, I am s-sorry." His head lolled back, his eyes went glassy. It was the last words he spoke.

Salena sobbed, nodding vigorously as if she wholeheartedly agreed with her husband's scolding.

Having pulled himself up onto his knees to aim the deadly arrow at Duncan, John now tossed his longbow away and collapsed at Catriona's side. His body trembled and perspired uncontrollably. Never before had he pushed himself to this level of energy-expending exhaustion, not even that first day he had healed two mortal wounds in Catriona's chest. Nausea and dizziness plagued him, making him groan and flail about. Fatigue engulfed him, and he finally welcomed the blessed embrace of sleep...or after all those centuries, was it finally death?

* * * * *

When Catriona came to awareness, she instantly knew she was cradled by the soothing coolness of snow. She sighed as she stirred and stretched, savoring the last bits of sleep with her eyes still closed. But it did not take long for her to remember...the unbearable pain and excruciating heat of fire, a fire that had apparently ebbed. Had she died at Duncan's cruel hand and gone to heaven? It must be so, she mused as she wiggled her foot, for her broken leg no longer throbbed, and her skin felt soft, cold and free of pain. She pulled in a long breath of air, testing her lungs. Ah, and they no longer burned from the thick smoke!

"Catriona..."

Her eyes flew open at the familiar voice. The pitch black of the night sky outlined Salena's beautiful form, her auburn hair fluttering in the wind like an archangel. As she knelt at Catriona's side, the dying coals of the fire near the camp Duncan had set flickered on the angles and smooth planes of Salena's face. Her stark blue eyes glistened with tears, and she released her frown to display a trembling, relieved smile.

"Oh, Catriona, you live!" Salena breathed, running her cool hands over Catriona's face and arms.

Her gaze flicked to the red mark at Salena's neck. "Hinny, h-how did ye get that nasty cut on yer neck?"

Salena slapped her hand across the wound and glanced to her side where Catriona now spotted Falcon. "'Tis not important. Catriona, love, are you well enough to rise?"

"Rise? But how did ye both get here to—" She lifted her head and twisted her body until she caught sight of the pale form lying motionless in a pool of blood near the campsite. She sucked in a sharp breath. "Is that…"

"Aye, 'tis Duncan," Falcon offered, pacing back and forth through the snow. To Salena, he urged, "We must hurry, love."

"W-what's goin' on here? Is Duncan d-dead?"

Salena took Catriona's cold hands in hers. "Do you not recall? Duncan tied you to that tree," she said hurriedly, indicating the smoking, charred yew tree nearby. "He burned you…almost to death. We found you just in time."

The whole incident swam through her mind making her dizzy. Renewed anger at her deceptive husband boiled up within her soul. She clenched her hands into fists and thought of his crazed abuse and attempted murder of her. The past execution of her innocent mother by his zealous command fed Catriona's ire further. One by one, her mind ticked all his known transgressions off in an explosion of startling truths. Fraser's declaration of his own death by Duncan's orders came to the forefront of her thoughts as well. Every cruel confession Duncan had made since abducting her caused her heart to thump with fury and a need for vengeance. Her gaze shot to Duncan's lifeless form. But it looked as if she already had her revenge. She had never wanted to see him dead, and had deeply grieved his "death" almost one year ago. But he certainly had asked for what destiny had finally befallen him.

Finally, she rejoiced in true widowhood.

"Aye, I recall now, and God forgive me, but I am glad to see him dead."

"Very much understood. Now," Falcon said, his voice rushed, "we must make haste and depart this place."

"Depart? But…" She lifted her hands, sat bolt upright in the snow and patted her bare arms, her legs. "I-I am nude, and…och! I am not burned 'tall!" She sniffed, glancing down to see her long tresses now singed up to the level of her nipples. "With the exception of me hair."

"Aye, that was not his priority. He did not quite get to that."

"He?" Her eyes widened. Heedless of the cold against her completely naked body, Catriona leapt to her bare feet. "John—where is John? I say, do ye refer to John?"

Falcon turned and pointed to a group of steeds tethered at a nearby tree. John's unconscious body slumped over the bare back of one of the horses. "Aye, he is there. During the few minutes of your comatose recovery, I ran to fetch our mounts left behind just around the gully's bend. Seems John's powers were wholly spent after *invisilating* to your location and healing your extensive burns and battered body. In the many centuries of our acquaintance, I have never seen John so weary after use of his powers. He had to be carried and placed upon the stallion's back, and I...I fear for his welfare."

She remembered now, but knew if she had not been reminded, the event would have been lost to her foggy memories forever. The trauma of near-death had had her thinking she had hallucinated and imagined John, as if he had come to her as her savior, her angel shortly before all went black. But visions swam back to her of him spinning around her, dousing the fire with showering drifts of snow, even as excruciating agony engulfed her. She could remember the extreme relief of the icy cold numbing her blistered skin.

But Catriona would give her life up to that fire again if it meant John's restored health. She despaired at seeing him so vulnerable, and never wished to be the root of his distress and lethargy again!

"We do not have time for further exchange. We must be on our way posthaste. John requires our energizing services at once." Falcon raced to the group of horses, Salena close on his heels. He reached into two separate saddlebags and pulled out a pair of braies, a man's shirt, boots and a fur-lined cloak. He thrust the wad toward Salena. "Darling, assist her to dress quickly. Hurry, before she freezes...and before we lose John."

Catriona's heart galloped with fear. "Lose him? B-but he is immortal, he..." She stood stiff with alarm as Salena darted to her, held out the braies and helped Catriona to don them. Just hearing the verbal confirmation of her silent fears made it all the more real and frightening.

"Shh, Cat, please hasten at once! We must find shelter quickly. Kiss him as we travel to sustain him. But he needs our love and our full sexual energy very soon...or he could die."

Die? Her stomach pitched with anguish. "Nae!" she returned with conviction, her voice cracking as she struggled to suppress the tears. "He will not die! I will not allow it!" She snatched the boots from Salena and hurriedly slipped her feet into them. Without so much as a split-second pause, she jammed on the shirt and swirled the cloak around her body. Catriona took off in a sprint and hurdled up onto the horse behind John. Gathering him close, she shouted, "Come! We ride straightaway."

Salena and Falcon raced to their horses, propelling their bodies into the saddles. Catriona whirled the great stallion about, clamping her legs around John's hips, and took off in a thundering gallop behind Falcon and Salena.

# Chapter Nine

ဆာ

"Shelter!" Falcon murmured with a sigh, spurring his destrier onward.

The abandoned stable came into view at just the right moment. It was all Catriona could do to hold onto John's slumping form. Though Falcon had insisted as they traveled that he should ride with John, Catriona had adamantly refused, loath to release her lover despite her waning strength at keeping him mounted.

John moaned and twitched now and then. All she could do was stroke and soothe him, and urge her mount closer to a blessed haven. Twice during the half-hour-long ride, she had managed to coax him to sit up so she could give him an energizing kiss as they neared their destination. It had seemed to slightly sustain him, but even now as Falcon led them into the open doorway of the decrepit structure, John appeared once again to be fading back into that deep, dangerous chasm of delirium.

When they approached, Catriona slid off her horse. Following behind Falcon and Salena, she led her steed toward the gaping doorway. The moon broke through a brief break in the clouds at that very moment, and it was then she took note of John's pasty complexion. Drenched in sweat and listless, he appeared to be all but dead.

"Hurry, please hurry," Catriona cried, stepping inside as she took John's limp hand in hers.

Falcon had, by now, dismounted and was securing the door shut against the whistling winds. "If I but had John's powers of speed, believe me, I would be using them to their utmost degree," Falcon mumbled.

Near the door, Salena already had located and lit a lantern, and currently corralled her and Falcon's horses into a wide stall. On a steadfast mission, she crossed to a dilapidated strongbox at the rear of the barn and rooted through its contents. "Ah, perfect," she breathed, dragging piles of wool horse blankets, bed quilts and one huge bear fur from the coffer.

While Falcon strode to John's side and hauled him from the horse's back, Salena hung the lantern and set up a broad, cozy bed in a separate stall surrounded by heaps of clean straw. Catriona followed Falcon into the small fenced area, kneeling on the makeshift bed and wringing her hands in impatient worry.

"Oh, John, John…"

As soon as Falcon had John lying down on the fur, Catriona bent and closed her mouth over his. He groaned, his eyelids fluttering. At first, his lower body lay flaccid and unresponsive. Her mouth moved against his dry lips, her cheek abraded across his perspiring, whisker-roughened upper lip.

Now she could sense the slow and sure drawing of energy he took from her. An overpowering joy wrapped by relief leapt into her heart. He now barely moved his lips under hers, and she sighed into his mouth when his tongue flickered upward to stroke hers. It was when she felt the trembling expanse of his hand behind her head that she tore her lips from his and stared down into those crystal, mesmerizing orbs.

"John, ye are awake! Oh, darlin', I am so verra sorry I ran away and caused ye all this trouble." Unshed tears stung her eyes, threatening to spill over. She pressed one hand to his shadowed, stubbly cheek, reveling in the rough yet tingly sensation. "'Twas just that I never wished to be a burden or to impose any of me dangers upon ye or yer people."

"Shh, my love, I understand," he replied in a weak whisper, puffs of condensation rolling from his mouth and nose. "You must believe you have not caused a thing. 'Twas my smitten heart and destiny that are to blame."

"Damn yer blasted destiny!" she cried, hot tears raining down her cheeks. She slammed her mouth into his, imparting more strength into his soul. As she showered his face and lips with wet kisses, she murmured, "I would fight yer supposed fate tooth and blade to have ye as me mate, so it does not matter one wee whit who or what is to blame."

"Ah, ye *have* got me as yer mate, lass, do ye nae see?" He mimicked her Scottish burr, delighting her to no end. Reprieve washed through her in one cleansing, revitalizing sweep.

"Do ye nae ken I'll be holdin' ye to that proclamation, mon? And come to think on it, I've two who'll be bearin' witness to that fact." She jerked her gaze to Falcon and Salena whom at that very moment were engaged in a bit of lewd petting of their own near John's feet.

Still not completely rejuvenated, John slowly lifted his gaze until he located them. "Many humble thanks to you all."

"Mmm," Salena purred, leaning back into Falcon as he slid a hand into the bodice of her gown. "Your kind welcomes always go unsaid and without necessity. Now quit your chattering and let us get down to the matter at hand...restoring your energy with swift surety by a delicious foursome encounter."

"Hmm, seems you have turned into quite the harlot over the years, my love," Falcon growled as he nipped at her ear. "Oh, but I do *love* it!"

Catriona's heart raced with thoughts of the coming event. She did not know how she had become so lucky to have ended up as part of this glorious, carnal quadrangle. This amazing man had fast become the focus in her life, and the most important link in this concordant, breathtaking arrangement. She would gladly spend the rest of her life providing him the powers he needed to sustain his immortality whether by one-on-one lovemaking, or with Falcon and Salena included in their embrace for that compounded boost.

Now that the danger seemed to have subsided somewhat, she relaxed and allowed herself to study his sprawled form. Just one sweeping gaze sent her blood pumping all through her body, settling in an almost painful throb in her groin.

"I want ye somethin' fierce," she whispered as she trailed a hand over his thick chest. Her fingers brushed one of his nipples through his shirt.

The move promptly elicited a hiss from him.

"I want ye, me bandit, however I can get ye. I wish to gift ye with as much of those needed powers as I can muster. And I am verra willin' to include Falcon and Salena as needed to boost yer energy tenfold. Oh, John..." She choked it out, the tears flowing faster, harder. "I never want to see ye that close to death again!"

He yanked her down on his chest squeezing her tight, stroking her back so that shivers of delight shimmied up her spine. "Aye, I never wish to be in that situation again, either. But I would do it for you, Catriona. I would do it over and over just to keep you safe." John lifted her face, cupping it so that she was forced to look upon his impassioned expression. "I would die for you."

No one had ever said such a kind, loving thing to her before this profound moment! "Thank ye so verra much," she rasped, her cheeks wet against his palms. "Thank ye for comin' after me and savin' me from that vile man." She shuddered. "Ah, the pain, the horror he put so many people through..."

"Shh," John said, pressing a kiss to the tip of her nose. "'Tis over. Do not think of it or him ever again. You are safe now with me, and I wish to be energized by your bewitching charms."

"Oh, me chivalrous knight, yer every wish is me every decree!" She kissed him again, reaching down to unfasten his braies as she did so. Catriona was shocked and wantonly delighted to find that his cock already had filled to the point of half-erection. She pushed the garment down far enough to release the spongy tool from its prison, and closed her hand around its inviting girth. John let out an animal sound of pleasure, his eyelids fluttering with languid appreciation.

The stable had warmed somewhat due to the securing of the door, the piles of straw surrounding them, the many warm bodies in such close proximity and the fur and blankets for insulation. But due to the remaining chill in the air, Catriona knew this would be a haphazard, partially clothed lovemaking session. It did not disappoint her, though. Something about the almost spontaneous, hurried nature of it made her all the more excited. She glanced up to see Falcon releasing one of Salena's breasts from the bodice of her gown while keeping it on her for added warmth. He had her skirts lifted and currently plunged his fingers into her wet quim. Eager and hungry, she moaned and thrust her pelvis into his hand.

Catriona was aware and very pleased that the four of them would be connected in the moments to come. But for now, she wanted to taste John, to devour him and have him all to herself. She walked on her knees sidling up closer near his hip. Taking the silky rod in her hand, she studied its veiny surface, its thickness and long length that she knew very soon, would grow even larger. Toward the tip, the veins became less apparent, and it smoothed upward until it all came together at that one moistened slit. She tightened her grip, loving the deep, sexy sounds she wrought from him. Stroking once, twice, she marveled at how quickly it filled with blood and grew harder in her hand. Catriona licked her lips, hungry and greedy to taste his shaft. She bent and flicked her tongue around the tip.

"Jesus!" John hissed and tensed, but did not move away.

"I want to take ye in me mouth, John. Can I impart energy to ye in this manner, eat ye up and swallow ye whole?"

"I'm counting on it, baby," he said with rapid breaths, his thick hard chest rising and falling.

She did not engage him in any further conversation. Instead, she wrapped one hand around the base and opened her mouth, reaching up with her other hand to tweak his nipples through his shirt. His cock slid in past teeth, past tongue, right into her throat. She relaxed her throat muscles, taking him as deep as she could without gagging. Salty sweet flavors burst in her mouth. It felt much like sucking on a candy-coated, tubular stone. It made her thirsty and starved all at once. Ravenous now, she swirled her tongue around and around the head, sucking, licking, withdrawing, plunging back down again.

John held his breath, released it, held it again, cried out. "Ah, Cat, you sweet little harlot, you! Mmm, aye, just like that, darling, just like that."

With each kiss she had given him, and now each wave of pleasure he experienced, she knew his energies were building. Knowing she had such control, to be able to provide him with forces to sustain his immortal powers, it was the ultimate aphrodisiac to her. It made her pussy clench, throb and swell, and a damp trickle soaked the crotch of her braies.

After pleasuring him for several minutes while Falcon and Salena dropped to the fur beside John, Catriona released John's cock and stood.

John let out a groan of disappointment. "What are you doing? Please do not leave me like this, you minx."

Blood now warming her body to that of an inferno, she pushed her braies down and kicked them aside, welcoming the cool rush of air on her ass and wet lips. "I'm goin' to ride ye fast and hard, like I've never ridden anythin' before."

"Holy..." was all John could muster as he gazed up at her half-naked body framed by the cloak she still wore.

"Mmm-hmm, that sounds like an excellent idea." Salena maneuvered Falcon so that he lay parallel to John, so close their thick male arms touched. She lifted her skirts and straddled her husband, dragging her soaking cunt up and down over his huge cock jutting from the unfastened gap of his braies.

"Wife, you sure do know how to carry out your duties, that is for damn sure."

Salena giggled, lifted a coaxing hand and waved it at Catriona. "Come now, take John into your heart and let us give these outlaws a taste of their own mayhem."

Catriona grinned and laced her hand into Salena's. She knelt and straddled John, scooting up until her dripping vagina poised above the tip of his manhood. "Are ye ready to fuel yer sorcerer's spirit, me brigand, me Little John of Robin Hood's Merry Men?"

"Aye," he said hoarsely, his eyes glazed over with rabid passion. "More so than ever before in my entire existence."

Just by the kisses and fellatio, it seemed he had gained enough strength to guide her onto his erection. His big hands spanned her hips and lifted her until the tip aligned exactly with her hole. Tiny frissons of hot-cold pleasure shot off in her pussy, but he did not give her time to acclimate herself to the bliss. In one swift downward thrust, he had himself buried to the tip of her very womb.

"Oh my God!" Catriona twitched, amazed when the orgasm slammed into her. In this position, the massive girth and length of him stimulated nerves she did not even know existed. She could even feel her asshole spasming right along with her canal. White juices oozed out to soak the base of his cock and his sac.

"Ah, Cat," John whispered. "You are so sexy, so full of passion. I cannot believe I was lucky enough to find you that day running for your life across the meadow."

He drew her down and kissed her, his tongue tracing her lips then delving into her mouth. Now that the urgency had passed to force power into him, she allowed herself to taste the remnants of ale in his kiss. Everything about him intoxicated her, and she welcomed the aching return of desire to her loins as he reached up and kneaded her breasts. Her nipples were already hard pearls of need, but he tweaked and squeezed just right, making them pucker further and sending streaks of yearning through her blood. She moved on him, with him, as he rocked her, slowly stroking his cock in and out of her pussy.

"John, the connection..." Falcon said, his voice muffled.

Catriona glanced aside to see that Salena had crawled up Falcon's chest. She now sat on his face holding her skirts up in a huge wad at her belly. From her current angle, Catriona could see Salena's smooth ass and the back half of her pussy lips poised over Falcon's mouth. The sight made Catriona moan. She tried to imagine her cunt getting licked in the same dominant fashion, and marveled when a second orgasm threatened to slam into her.

Salena turned around at that moment so that she continued to sit astride Falcon's face, although she now could look into Catriona's eyes. "Aye, the connection." Her breathtaking blue gaze caught and held Catriona's. "Catriona, bend across and take Falcon's cock in your mouth."

She shot a quick glance at Falcon's enormous shaft jutting from his unfastened braies. It looked delicious, thick and throbbing, just as John's had been in her mouth. "B-but..."

"John needs the power. Remember how much our four-way link energized them both?"

Catriona nodded, her heart pounding not with opposition but with anticipation, for there was no doubt she would do just what Salena suggested. "Oh, aye, I recall with crystal clarity. Ye will be gettin' nae protest from the likes of me."

"Cat, honey, are you sure?" John asked gently, rubbing his hands up and down her arms so that she felt she might melt into him by the gentleness of his touch.

"Verra, verra sure. I owe me life to ye several times o'er."

"You do not have to do this as a debt repayment, the way we jested between one another that first day we met."

She rose up on her knees and scooted down toward his thighs, keeping his long cock inside her. The move silently instructed John to slide down so that the top of his head ended up level with Falcon's shoulder.

"What...are you doing?" he asked, but awareness flared in his eyes when she reached out and closed her palm around Falcon's cock.

"I do not do this to repay ye, John. I do it because...because I love ye with all me heart."

Salena stilled her dance above Falcon's face. Falcon lifted his head and peeped out from between his wife's legs. John's jaw dropped open, and elation glowed from his eyes, a heartwarming, smoldering radiance she had never seen in anyone else's eyes before this moment.

"Beg pardon, milady, but could you please repeat yourself?"

Catriona grinned. "Aye, I'll be repeatin' meself for the ol' immortal man whom apparently has lost his hearin'. I said I love ye. I do not ken how it happened so fast, but nonetheless, I love ye, John Lawton, with all me life, soul, heart and body. Why else would I be bendin' o'er," she said as she took Falcon's cock in her mouth, "and suckin' off another man's phallus with ye watchin'?"

A riotous collection of laughter rang out even as Catriona went to work. But it did not take long for Falcon's chuckles to evolve into moans. Which in turn, transformed into wet slurps as he dove into his wife's moist slit while receiving oral pleasures on his own organ.

In gleeful shock, all John could do was grip Catriona's waist and slide her up and down on his cock while she maintained that energizing bond between the four of them. Ah, to be filled with John's enormous penis while feasting on another in her mouth, it had to be complete wickedness straight from the devil. The sweet flavors and sinful sensations bombarded her from both ends. The fullness in her mouth and pussy, coupled with the heat of two men's bodies, made her sigh and suck harder. She could hear Salena's high-pitched, sexy moans and gasps as Falcon continued to gorge on her little pussy. The scent of straw wafted up to mix with that of musky sex juices and warm flesh. The flickering lantern cast a soft yellow glow on them all, forming shadows in the folds of clothing and a light sheen across shimmering flesh.

John's strong hands guided her hips, plunging her harder and faster onto his shaft. She relaxed the muscles in her neck and took Falcon further into her throat. That was when Salena bent forward, her cunt still being delved by Falcon's tongue, and hunched so that she could watch Catriona suck off her husband.

"Mmm, may I join you?" she purred.

The question perplexed Catriona at first, but then she watched with renewed lust as Salena reached down and around Catriona's head to cup her husbands balls. Falcon let out a deep and torturous, muffled cry.

"Keep doing what you are doing. I will handle these," Salena assured her with a wink. And she stretched so that she could draw one side of his sac and marble into her mouth.

Falcon screamed this time, writhing and bucking, his head raising and reaching for his wife. His arms slapped around Salena's hips so that he could hold her retreating pussy to his mouth. Salena moaned and thrust her cunt against his face while drawing his balls further into her mouth. Catriona bucked on John's cock as the urge to suck Falcon harder and faster overtook her. John plucked up her free hand where she had been reaching out to his chest to caress his sculpted muscles through the garment. He lifted his head and took first one finger, then two and three into his mouth. Tingly fire shot from the tips of her fingers, up her arm and straight down to her pussy where his cock nestled.

Barraged by myriad carnal sensations, Catriona was certain she had reached the utmost echelon of pleasure in her entire life. She reached for that summit of release, her body sensing the tight draw of it, like thin leather stretched taut across a drum. But she soon realized that tantalizing echelon had further unseen heights in its midst. While John pounded upward into her, animalistic growls and howls escaping through his clenched teeth, she went higher still, almost arriving there at the crown of her climax. The desperate reaching only made her suck harder and faster on Falcon's cock, one hand stroking him in rhythm with her mouth's movements, the other still being ravished by John's talented mouth.

Then it happened all at once. Tiny bursts of pleasure exploded in her loins, sending her catapulting far above even the highest pike imaginable. She screamed out her astonished pleasure, her response muted by her full mouth. Catriona sensed Falcon's climax by the stiffening of his body right before the warm, sticky cum shot down her throat. Salena twitched, her shoulder bumping against Catriona's head as she continued to suckle Falcon's scrotum during her own violent release.

"Catriona...oh, holy Zeus of gods!" John's cry of ecstasy came out stifled by her fingers. He yanked his mouth from the digits and sat up even as he spilled his seed deep into her womb. Dragging her off Falcon so that she sat astride him, John crushed her to him so that their chests pressed together nipples to nipples.

Catriona loved the way he massaged her back and nuzzled her neck while the last remnants of the orgasm lingered. "John..." she whispered, kissing his mouth and cheeks as she raked her hands through his long hair. "Are ye better now?"

"Aye, amazing! I am completely invigorated, more so than ever in my entire existence. Falcon?"

"Mmm," he sighed, spent and still lying in opposite positions with his wife. Salena lay on Falcon's abdomen, her head turned to the side as she stared lovingly at his penis. Her spread legs flanked his head. "I do not think I will ever have to energize myself again," Falcon added.

John's mouth curved up into a roguish grin, but he turned back to gaze upon Catriona. His expression sobered. "Cat..." He kissed her, tucking a blanket around her bare legs when she shivered. "I cannot believe you have not run scared from me as other women have in the past. My large...tool," he explained glancing down to where their bodies still joined, "has been a source of fear and subsequent flight in many a women. And here you sit taking it all in without so much as a flinch—nay, *enjoying* it! Ah, and my Cat, I will never forget the sound of your husky voice professing your love to me this night. It will forever be etched in my heart. So it is with great sentiment and passion that I confess something to you."

His words took her breath away. While she could not see how any woman could reject such a delicious man, and she longed to hear more of these tales of women running frightened from his bed, she needed to hear that confession more. "What have ye done now, John Lawton, that'll be requirin' a declaration of guilt?"

Those eyes, as stark and alluring as sin, beheld her gaze. "I have done nothing but love you. Catriona Graham," he repeated, "I will love you until the day we must depart at the dreaded time of your death—nay, I will love you forever into eternity, whether you are alive or have since mortally passed on."

She gasped and stared agog at him, her heart doing all sorts of flips and joyful twists. But there was not time for her to respond or to react any further. The barn door burst open, and through the slats of the stalls, Catriona could see that a dark figure stood silhouetted against the sudden moonlight beyond. Robes flapped violently in the winds. Resentful at such a bold invasion upon this most intimate, memorable moment, Catriona knew without a doubt the intruder's identity. She withdrew herself from John, a sense of emptiness in its wake, and donned her braies in preparation to hear the bad news she sensed would come.

# Chapter Ten

**ꙮ**

"Lorcan! What the devil are you doing here?" John rose and fastened his pants. Falcon did the same, followed by Salena smoothing and righting her skirts and cloak. They all stepped out of the stall and into the center of the barn as Lorcan floated inside, staff clutched in his feeble hand. As if by magic, the door slammed shut behind him.

He crossed to Catriona, his white eyes only on her as he moved, the faint yellow glow of the lantern flickering on his weathered old face. A horrid sense of trepidation took hold of Catriona's heart and would not let go.

"I once said to you I would return when it is time..."

"Aye." She recalled the vivid dream as if it were moments ago. And she would not forget the horror of Duncan haunting that same nightmare. Cruel butterflies rushed around in her abdomen. Did he mean it was time for her to die, and so soon after she and John had declared their love for one another?

"It is time. I am completely certain of it now. Aye, I had my moments when I doubted your place as John's intended, but the *Scorpian* called to me not seconds past. It came much quicker with Salena, but with you...things stood in the way to cloud my judgment and the spell."

"Things?" John asked stepping up to drape an arm over Catriona's shoulders and draw her to his side.

"The husband, for one. This Duncan's time had to pass, leaving her a true widow prior to Catriona becoming fully yours. She had to be permanently free of him. Her vows had been spoken to him under pretext, yet the tie still needed to be severed."

"Aye, but he died hours ago."

"Mmm," Lorcan interjected, raising a gnarled finger in protest. "But there were further conditions to be met. Neither of you had yet declared your love to one another. Do not ask me how, but the *Scorpian*—and the *Centaurus*, as well—is aware of these things. My own haphazard spell seems to have its own rules. With it goes this *Scorpian* I have worn around my neck for decades," he continued, lifting from his chest the pendant with the striking green stone at its center, "which has now led me here to you...to Catriona."

"To me?" Catriona recalled Salena's words regarding the *Scorpian* matching her eyes. Was it true? Was this her destiny, to be John's intended? The mere notion of it elated her to jubilant tears.

She thought of the dream again, struggled to remember Lorcan's profound, cryptic words. *Oh, Catriona Graham of Scotland afar, to avoid the bloodshed of hatred and war. Your gift and your heart, your pillar of life, 'twill lead to an eternity as your chosen one's wife.*

"To you," Lorcan said huskily, stepping up to her. She was taller than he, and she had to look down into his upturned, wrinkled face. He lifted the long gold chain over his head, placed it around her neck and turned the pendant so it faced him. The stone glowed and flashed as if sealing fate. It nestled cool and yet warm between her breasts. She experienced an immediate tingly sensation, and a great sense of power and invincibility raced throughout her whole body.

"'Tis that simple? I-I am now immortal?" she asked, stunned.

"Aye, and bound to John as long as you wear the pendant. But I warn you, do not ever remove it or attempt to test its powers."

"So you were right, old man," John said with a somewhat astonished tone. "All these years you have claimed my intended would enter my life, yet you did not know how, when or who."

Lorcan sighed, and Catriona thought he looked much older and wearier than when she had first seen him in her dream. He trembled and tears pooled in his white eyes.

"It was not until the *Scorpian* drew me here just now that I was sure. I have done my best over the centuries to decipher my own antidote spell cast on the medallions in hope of counteracting Desmona's eternal curse. A curse, mind you, that has not only damned me to this old man's body, but riddled me with a daft and scatterbrained mind."

"Desmona?" Falcon asked.

"Aye, the witch who—" Suddenly, the *Scorpian* pulsed and glowed, momentarily blinding them. The beam reached out from its place nestled in Catriona's cleavage and struck Lorcan in the chest. He fell to his knees upon the dirt-packed floor of the stable clutching the crystal staff for support.

"Lorcan!" Both John and Falcon shouted in unison, dropping to the ground on either side of him.

But his complete form was no longer discernable. A dusty golden cloud spun up and around Lorcan, enveloping him in an impermeable cylinder that Catriona's hand could not breach when she attempted to reach for him. Salena tried, as well, and looked up at Catriona with alarm when her fingers seemed to hit a wall.

The cocoon spun around Lorcan faster and faster while he remained kneeling on the dirt floor of the stable. The many nooks and crannies of the barn were filled by its glowing light. It finally spun upward into nothingness, and as it did so, it drew up a drapery of sorts, leaving behind a form hunched on the floor. It was Lorcan in some ways, yet not Lorcan at all. The staff had disappeared. All that remained of the previous likeness of Lorcan was the clothing.

"L-Lorcan?" Salena murmured.

"Lorcan, are you all—" But John's words were cut short when the figure slowly raised its head.

"Wait a minute, what in the hell..." Falcon got to his feet and stared down at the pale-haired head that knelt before him.

The thin shoulders shook, and Catriona heard the pitiful sobs. She dropped to her knees in front of this strange Lorcan, and tilted the chin further up with a bent finger. What met her stare had her gasping along with Falcon, John and Salena.

"Who are ye?" Catriona asked.

Gray eyes the very color of an ominous, oncoming storm cloud met her gaze. Tears spilled down high cheekbones onto the feminine features of an ethereal goddess. Full pink lips trembled, and Catriona thought she had never seen such a gorgeous creature in her life. The person straightened then, confirming Catriona's suspicions. Aye, it was a woman, as evidenced by the ample breasts that strained against the dark brown robes the wizard Lorcan had always worn.

"I-I-I am a woman again!" Her voice came out in a soft, female tone, almost little-girl-like, and not at all in the gruff, deep manner of the old man Lorcan. Though the tears continued to fall, the plump lips curved into a smile of pure elation and wonder. A row of perfect white teeth glistened between the lips.

"Bloody hell, *what* is going on here?" That from John as he dragged himself up off the floor. He now looked down warily upon a woman where once there had been a man—a man who had been his lifelong, fatherlike mentor.

"Aye, I second that inquiry," Falcon put in. "What the fuck is going on here, Lorcan—or whoever the hell you are?"

The woman held out both hands, one to John, one to Falcon. They assisted her to her feet. She stood at an average height, somewhere a few inches in between that of Catriona's tall form and Salena's petite one. Her luxurious locks of pale hair billowed down her back in glorious waves. Catriona knew without confirmation that this woman, who had been masquerading somehow as an elderly man for a very long time, was of royal descent, despite the old robes she wore.

"I am Lorana Spenser, daughter of the very late Baron Warwick Spenser of Yorkshire. My mother was the illegitimate daughter of King Richard the first of England, and a woman reputed to be a witch. This had been a fact that had spurred much discord within the royal kingdom...and eventually with my nemesis, Desmona."

"Lorana?" Falcon asked, his golden eyebrows furrowed as he focused on that one perplexing name. "But we have been calling you Lorcan for centuries."

Lorana sighed, her pale eyes darkening. "That would be due to Desmona. She taunted me with 'Lorana can, Lorana cannot', in reference to my ability to release myself from her hex. The name Lorcan eventually stuck due to her persuasive and mischievous nature, and because it seemed better fitting an old wizard man than Lorana did."

"But who is this Desmona, and why would she taunt ye so and change ye into an elderly gent?" Catriona's curiosity had gotten the better of her, and she made the prompt decision to appease it.

Lorana's delicate jaw clenched. "She is an evil, vengeful sorceress who has held me under her spell for nearly four centuries. The only worthy thing about the hex proved to be that of becoming mentor over Falcon and John, and seeing all the good they have done over the generations. I suppose it served to soothe my maternal instincts raging within, as well."

John chuckled, drawing Catriona close. "I must say I am in shock that a beautiful maiden has been hidden all this time beneath that wrinkled old skin."

"By Jove, you can say that again!" Falcon interjected with a snort.

"Well," Salena said softly, taking Lorana by the hand, "we all thank you for the part you have played in our love matches, and we welcome you back and wish for your future happiness."

"Thank you," Lorana whispered, a tone of humbleness in her feminine voice.

"Ah, well then, Lorcan—er, Lorana," John supplied cheerily, "you will have to tell us the whole tale of this Desmona character over supper. Shall we all depart and *invisilate* to Sedgewick Castle?" He stretched and grinned sheepishly. "I definitely have more than enough energy to do so."

Falcon threw his head back and guffawed. He slapped John on the back. "Eh, after all that spicy lovemaking, you should be set for eternity!"

They all chuckled, including Lorana. "'Tis true, you should. And I should well know, for part of my torture was to have to watch all that delicious lovemaking, yet be deprived of it myself."

Falcon's mouth hung open. "You watched us this whole time? You poor thing."

"I…" Lorana's pale complexion pinkened, but despite her apparent embarrassment, she snorted. "I am the most sexually educated virgin to ever walk the face of this world."

Collective laughter filled the barn.

Catriona's giggles died down when something caught her eye. "Och! What is that there in yer robe?" She pointed to Lorana's chest. Beneath the surface of her garments, a lump stuck up. Light glowed through the layers of fabric.

Lorana's gaze fell and she gawked at the protuberance. Her hand shook as she traced its outline.

Salena went behind her and pushed aside Lorana's hair. "'Tis a chain with something attached." She pulled on the necklace until the object emerged out of the neckline. Walking around Lorana so that she could face her, Salena held the jewel in her hand and cooed, "Oh my, 'tis a gorgeous pendant with a sparkling amber stone."

Lorana's gaze rose, and Catriona saw that tears filled her eyes. "Thank the Lord, my spell has finally given me my

*Sagitar,*" she nodded. "It means that Desmona's curse could be nearing its end."

"*Sagitar?*"

"Aye," Lorana sniffed, the tears now streaming down her cheeks. "'Tis my destiny's key. Soon, I pray my antidote spell will finally free me of Desmona's cruel hex. If I conjured it up correctly all those centuries ago, I should now find *my* soul mate with the *Sagitar,* and then this whole long nightmare will be behind me."

She suddenly gasped, her gaze snapping from one to other. "But please, you all must remember… Should Desmona ever come to you, do not reveal to her my remedy spell and the medallions' roles in breaking her curse. All three medallions must remain a secret from that vile bitch until my mate has been found and I have been released from her powers. That is the blessed day I will finally rejoice in my own revenge."

# Epilogue
*One month later*

&

"Mmm, aye, me gorgeous husband, just like that," Catriona purred, arching her back.

They lay before the blazing fire in their suite at Sedgewick Castle. Falcon and Salena had long since returned to Wyngate Hall outside London, but Lorana had chosen to stay on at John's manor for the time being. The early March winds whistled around the keep, but their fortress of endless love within the chambers kept the newlyweds safe and warm.

John circled his tongue around her taut nipple once again, driving her to madness and making her pussy engorge with blood. She hissed and fisted her hands into the bear rug she lay on.

Catriona pulled in a deep breath and savored the mixed scents of burning wood, all-male heat and sexual arousal. He skimmed a hot hand down her abdomen and traced her clitoris with a slow-moving, butterfly-light fingertip. As his mouth bypassed the *Scorpian* — her immortal lifeline — which lay nestled between her globes, he moved over to suckle at her other breast. When he pinched one lip of her labia between his fingers and stretched it up and away from her hole, her eyes widened at the new tactic. The pain-pleasure sensation made her groan and wriggle under his touch. He repeated the same procedure on the other lip, following that torturous new talent with the sinking of one long finger into her wet cunt.

"Oh!"

"Ah, Cat, I cannot ever get enough of you. You are far beyond sweetness and utter perfection." He pumped her pussy, tracing his tongue under the curve of one breast, moving down further still across ribs, navel. Shivers of delight raced across her flesh.

"Well," she panted, "ye'll be havin' an eternity to try yer best to get enough, love."

"Never!" he vowed, and between his teeth, he nipped the skin stretched over her hipbone. "I love you, Catriona Lawton. I will never tire of you, my Gypsy."

She groaned. "And I will never tire of ye, me thief. I love ye with all of me—"

He closed his mouth over her sex and stole her breath—nay, her heart!—from her chest. She bucked up against him, basking in the hot wetness that stroked her folds. Her hands stabbed into his hair, tangling in the long, thick mass of midnight silk. The fire at her right crackled in time with the snaps of pleasure that burst in her pussy. A log shifted and sizzled, ashes rising into the flue just when he shoved that finger deeper, adding a second to the outer ring of her anus. He circled his fingertip around the tight hole using drippings from her cunt to moisten it for entry. But when he slowly sank the digit into her ass, the other finger still in her vagina as he continued to devour her clit, she thought she had died and gone to heaven. A heavy, languid wash of desire engulfed her, followed by a desperate, sudden urge to slam herself up against him. She lifted her hips and bucked upward, crying out when sparks of lust licked at her womb and deep into her rectum. He groaned and slurped, loath to release her from this tormenting ecstasy.

It did not take long. The hot slickness of his tongue lapped back and forth over her nub, and the more she reached for him, the more he increased the pressure. It sent her swiveling up into a plume of violent, smoky hunger. She rode the smoldering cloud, her vision blurring, her lungs burning, as she traversed the very edges of heaven. Catriona suddenly stilled her frenzied dance and a ragged breath caught in her throat. The climax exploded in her like gunpowder igniting inside a cannon. The muscles in her ass and pussy convulsed around his fingers, sweet ecstasy spattering her as if her burning body lay beneath a welcoming torrent of rain. She showered his tongue and stubbled chin with her milky cream. Deep, yet high-pitched moans carried throughout the chamber in a lover's song of joy.

John was ravenous, she knew by the crazed gleam in his vivid blue eyes. He nearly clawed his way up her body, his naked chest inflating and deflating with his impatience. "I have to get inside you, Cat—" he entered her in one long, violent stroke, "now."

"Oh, bloody hell," she rasped, hooking her ankles behind him. "Ye're so big!"

"Too late, wife." He panted as he pummeled her, in, out, deeper, harder. He pushed up onto his knees taking her with him so that she straddled him in an upright position. She nearly swooned when the firelight danced over the aroused expression on his handsome face. "You are stuck with me and my huge cock for eternity."

She would never be able to get enough of his thick girth and length, even in this erotic position with her weight pressing down firmly upon his tool. Catriona gripped the solid meat of his shoulders and slammed downward, grinding her clit against his pubic bone. His hands clenched her ass cheeks, the fingers biting into her mounds. He bent and kissed her neck making shivers of delight rumble through her blood. The kisses turned to sucking, then nipping. He growled and she felt his cock twitch inside her, a sure sign he hovered near his peak.

One hand came down on her bare rear in a sharp smack while the other continued to clench her flesh.

"Oh!" She gasped, surprise making her head snap back. She looked into the eyes of a wild animal at the very second the pain eased into pleasure. Trails of heat led from the point of contact on her ass to deep inside her loins. The fire on her buttocks had turned into some sort of wanton drug in a matter of seconds. She welcomed the warm, sticky discharge from her pussy. It pooled out around the base of his cock and dribbled onto his swollen sac. And Catriona knew at that moment her husband was introducing her to yet another hedonistic pleasure.

"Again. Do it again." Her voice came out breathy, pleading.

"Mmm." He smacked the other cheek, his teeth grinding together. "I am going to—aw, hell, I cannot hold back!"

The orgasm engulfed her as his hot cum filled her womb. She bounced up and down, drawing out the pleasure, focusing on the pain that continued to burn on her rear. It seemed to go on and on, both of them struggling to hold tight to one another as their bodies jerked and twitched. She felt the unmistakable sensation of John absorbing energy from her, and nothing in this world pleased her more than giving such a gift to her forever lover.

They fell in a tangled heap on the fur, John murmuring soft, sexy words of love in her ear as he nuzzled her neck, kissed her earlobe, stroked her sensitive breasts.

A knock sounded at the door.

John raised his head. "Who goes there?"

"'Tis I, Lorana," came the soft voice.

He sighed and set Catriona from him. To her, he murmured, "Don your nightrail," as he wrapped a linen sheet around his hips, then bent and jammed on his braies. To Lorana, he raised his voice and barked, "Enter!"

The arched oak door swung slowly open. Even after the month since Lorana's transformation, Catriona's breath still caught in her lungs upon sight of Lorana. Her brilliant, almost pastel beauty could only belong to that of a princess. The long undulating locks of her flaxen hair spread around her lithe, feminine curves like the cape of a queen. She wore a burgundy, fur-lined cloak under its glorious spill, and Catriona could see that she had donned a sturdy black day dress beneath. The *Sagitar* dangled between her full breasts glittering golden in the languid light of the room. As Lorana glided further into the room, her silver eyes startling against the paleness of her heart-shaped face, Catriona caught a hint of her sweet, almost innocent essence.

"Forgive my intrusion at this hour, my lord," she said almost as if she were a peasant in awe of her master. Her delicate girl-like voice sang in direct opposition to her fully ripe body, sure evidence she was all woman. "'Tis just that a very important matter has arisen."

John blinked and strode up to her. "Lorana, what it is? Are you all right?"

She nodded, one hand reaching out to grip John's arm. "Aye, I am fine. 'Tis just that..." Lorana spun and crossed to the fire, looking down on the very spot where they had just made love. The firelight danced upon the smooth planes of her face casting her in an angelic light. She reached up and fondled the *Sagitar*, and from her place at Lorana's left side, Catriona could see her eyes searching far into the flames beyond the stone hearth.

"Lorana, are ye ill?" Catriona flew to Lorana and set a firm hand on her shoulder. She pressed her palm to Lorana's forehead, but the skin felt cool to the touch.

"Nay." She lifted her gaze, swung it slowly toward Catriona. Unshed tears filled the smoky orbs. "But I must go. Now."

"Go?" John took quick strides across the room and flanked her other side. "Where? Why? Lorana, what has happened to make you insist on departing so abruptly—and at this hour of the night?"

Her lips thinned. She lifted the *Sagitar* and thrust it toward John. "This. This is why. It calls to me, a spell of my own making, tempting me beyond endurance. It calls me to my soul mate whom I do not even know. I cannot fight the medallion's pull any longer. I cannot even wait until sunrise, the lure is so fierce. It tells me to go at this very moment, to follow my heart and not stop until I find him. So I must."

John started to protest, but his jaw snapped shut in resistance. "Very well, then I will call upon Lance, Berwyk and Aric to escort you indefinitely."

"Nay, 'tis not necessary. Have you forgotten I am immortal too, with powers of my own? Just because I am female does not mean I cannot fend for myself."

John blinked. "I see...well then, how about simply for company? You cannot be left unaided out there in that nasty world. And I do not wish you to become lonesome."

Lorana smiled, the warmth and affection reaching her glistening eyes. She pressed her palm to his cheek and stared up into his eyes. "Your concern warms my heart, John. I readily admit my own concern for you and Falcon was haphazard due to Desmona's spell. So to have the care and worry I attempted to show you and Falcon over the centuries returned to me means more than you will ever know." The tears trickled down her ivory cheeks, but the smile remained on her face. "I pray you both have known that I have loved you like you were my own sons. That I will always love you."

John inhaled and drew her into his arms, his breath coming out in a resigned groan. "Aye, your love was always apparent, despite Lorcan's peculiar ways." He pressed a kiss on top of her head. "And Falcon and I always returned that love and affection in our own curious way."

Lorana squeezed him tight and quickly withdrew. She scurried toward the door. "I must go now. I will visit you all on occasion. Please give Falcon and Salena my love." With her hand on the doorknob, she slid her gaze to Catriona. "And to you, as well, Catriona. I will always be indebted to both you and Salena for your parts in breaking down this spell."

Catriona nodded. "'Twas me pleasure. Godspeed to ye."

Lorana merely bowed her head and backed from the room, closing the door softly behind her.

Catriona wound her arms around John's neck and pressed her cheek against his thick chest. Lorana's unique, faint scent of sweet ginger still clung to John's clothing. Catriona inhaled its aroma, feeling a great sense of indebtedness to Lorana for her part in their happiness. She was so grateful to have happened upon John that day weeks ago, and glad that she did not have that long journey of searching for love ahead of her as Lorana did.

"John?"

"Hmm?"

"How long do ye suppose it will take her to find her intended mate?"

His breast expanded as he drew in a lengthy, deep breath. "She may not realize it or wish to face it, but my feeling is that Desmona is not through with Lorana yet. Aye, I suspect it will be a long, cruel journey before Lorana finally finds her mate and is released from the spell...if ever."

Catriona kissed him, loving the gentle giant she had been bound to by destiny. When she felt the stirrings of his cock through the thickness of her nightrail and his braies, she decided she would wait until a better time to tell him of her recent séance encounter. During meditation earlier that day, the spirit of a dead man had come to her adamantly demanding to speak with Lorana. Within seconds, she had lost the connection, leaving her wondering if she had imagined it.

But right this moment, Catriona knew she did not imagine the huge erection pressing into her abdomen. Aye, she would inform her husband of the strange spirit contact at a more appropriate moment when passion was not stealing the very voice from her soul.

*The End*

# Why an electronic book?

We live in the Information Age—an exciting time in the history of human civilization, in which technology rules supreme and continues to progress in leaps and bounds every minute of every day. For a multitude of reasons, more and more avid literary fans are opting to purchase e-books instead of paper books. The question from those not yet initiated into the world of electronic reading is simply: *Why?*

1. *Price.* An electronic title at Ellora's Cave Publishing and Cerridwen Press runs anywhere from 40% to 75% less than the cover price of the exact same title in paperback format. Why? Basic mathematics and cost. It is less expensive to publish an e-book (no paper and printing, no warehousing and shipping) than it is to publish a paperback, so the savings are passed along to the consumer.

2. *Space.* Running out of room in your house for your books? That is one worry you will never have with electronic books. For a low one-time cost, you can purchase a handheld device specifically designed for e-reading. Many e-readers have large, convenient screens for viewing. Better yet, hundreds of titles can be stored within your new library—on a single microchip. There are a variety of e-readers from different manufacturers. You can also read e-books on your PC or laptop computer. (Please note that Ellora's Cave does not endorse any specific brands.

You can check our websites at www.ellorascave.com or www.cerridwenpress.com for information we make available to new consumers.)

3. *Mobility.* Because your new e-library consists of only a microchip within a small, easily transportable e-reader, your entire cache of books can be taken with you wherever you go.

4. *Personal Viewing Preferences.* Are the words you are currently reading too small? Too large? Too... ANNOYING? Paperback books cannot be modified according to personal preferences, but e-books can.

5. *Instant Gratification.* Is it the middle of the night and all the bookstores near you are closed? Are you tired of waiting days, sometimes weeks, for bookstores to ship the novels you bought? Ellora's Cave Publishing sells instantaneous downloads twenty-four hours a day, seven days a week, every day of the year. Our webstore is never closed. Our e-book delivery system is 100% automated, meaning your order is filled as soon as you pay for it.

Those are a few of the top reasons why electronic books are replacing paperbacks for many avid readers.

As always, Ellora's Cave and Cerridwen Press welcome your questions and comments. We invite you to email us at Comments@ellorascave.com or write to us directly at Ellora's Cave Publishing Inc., 1056 Home Avenue, Akron, OH 44310-3502.

# COMING TO A BOOKSTORE NEAR YOU!

# ELLORA'S CAVE

*Bestselling Authors Tour*

UPDATES AVAILABLE AT

# WWW.ELLORASCAVE.COM

 erridwen, the Celtic Goddess of wisdom, was the muse who brought inspiration to storytellers and those in the creative arts. Cerridwen Press encompasses the best and most innovative stories in all genres of today's fiction. Visit our site and discover the newest titles by talented authors who still get inspired - much like the ancient storytellers did, once upon a time.

# Cerridwen Press

www.cerridwenpress.com